The Shadow in Renegade Basin

A Western Trio

The Shadow in Renegade Basin

A Western Trio

LES SAVAGE, JR.

Thorndike Press • Chivers Press
Thorndike, Maine USA   Bath, England

This Large Print edition is published by Thorndike Press, USA and by Chivers Press, England.

Published in 2001 in the U.S. by arrangement with Golden West Literary Agency

Published in 2001 in the U.K. by arrangement with Golden West Literary Agency

U.S. Hardcover 0-7862-3096-7   (Western Series Edition)
U.K. Hardcover 0-7540-4435-1   (Chivers Large Print)
U.K. Softcover 0-7540-4436-X   (Camden Large Print)

The text of this Large Print edition is unabridged.
Other aspects of the book may vary from the original edition.

Set in 16 pt. Plantin by Minnie B. Raven.

Printed in the United States on permanent paper.

British Library Cataloguing-in-Publication Data available

Library of Congress Cataloging-in-Publication Data
Savage, Les.
    The shadow in Renegade Basin : a western trio /
Les Savage, Jr.
    Contents: Plunder Trail — Brand of Penasco — The shadow
in Renegade Basin.
    p. cm.
    ISBN 0-7862-3096-7 (lg. print : hc : alk. paper)
    1. Western stories. I. Title.
PS3569.A826 A6   2001
    813'.54—dc21   00-051181

Table of Contents

Plunder Trail

Les Savage, Jr.'s title for this short novel was more descriptive than dramatic or evocative — "Oregon Traitor Trail." Malcolm Reiss, senior editor at Fiction House, bought the story in early October, 1943, originally intending to run it in *Lariat Story Magazine*. Instead, it appeared under the title "Plunder Trail" in *Frontier Stories* (Summer, 1944), another Fiction House magazine that Reiss edited. The author was paid $330.00 for it upon acceptance. In this, its first appearance since initial magazine publication, the text of the story has been restored according to the author's typescript, although the magazine title for it has been retained.

One ☗

The gilt-edged bat-wing doors of Omaha's Diamond Hall swung shut behind Ed Manton, and he stood there a moment, wearily letting the familiar sounds roll over him. The clink of glasses, the muted slap of cards, the dull voice calling keno numbers from somewhere upstairs — all so much a part of his years along the Missouri River.

Manton's gray eyes swept the room indifferently, and he wouldn't have needed to look. The men might have been all cut from the same pattern and scattered up and down the Missouri from New Orleans to the British Territories. There was the red-faced barman, wiping half-heartedly at the mahogany bar with its stacks of cut glass and bowls of pretzels. There were the inevitable tail-coated percentage dealers who worked for the house, a couple of them nibbling at the free lunch. By a cuspidor stood a long, lean man in foxed California pants and fancy-topped Justins.

Manton shrugged off his weary disgust. It was his life, and he would never be free of it.

He'd seen others of his kind try to change, knights of the green cloth, with magic in their fingers and the deadly fascination for the pasteboards in their blood. Some men were born gamblers, and nothing but death would take them away from the cards.

Manton moved into the haze of stale cigar smoke, past the crowd around the two billiard tables that stood opposite the bar, toward the stairs that led to the gambling tables on the second floor. He was a tall man, big shoulders filling out a black claw-hammer coat that hung about dark wool pants. His whole face was held in a careful mask that had been cultivated through the years until it was habitual and permanent, and, where there might have been a pleasing mobility in his broad mouth, there was only a stiff, unyielding line; where his eyes might have been bright steel, beneath their craggy brows, they were only dull, gray veils that hid whatever went on behind them.

A roulette table stood in the center of the upstairs room, a keno game going on to one side, several faro layouts on the other. Manton moved toward the row of round deal tables standing along the rear wall, with a series of doors behind them that marked the private salons. He caught up with a quartet of men walking toward one of those doors.

"Room for another, Drago?" he asked the sallow-faced dealer.

Drago turned, unable to hide the impatience that flickered through his bloodshot eyes. "Don't think so, Manton. Private game."

"It ain't that private," said a bearded youth. "You can sit in as far as I'm concerned, stranger. My name's Nestor. Bart Nestor."

"Manton," said the gambler, accepting the strong handshake, "Ed Manton."

Nestor's heavy, black beard couldn't hide the youth in his face. His homespun trousers and tan hickory jacket were thick with trail dust. Manton had seen enough emigrants passing through Omaha on the Oregon Trail to mark one here. The dull-eyed Drago halted and turned, hitching at one of the garters holding up the sleeve of his striped shirt.

"Now, look here, Nestor, I thought you wanted a private room," he said testily.

"I told you that it was all right with me," grinned the big youth, "but that doesn't mean nobody else can sit in. The more playing, the more money to win is what I always say." He laughed cheerfully.

Drago's mouth twisted angrily, then he spun on his heel and walked stiffly toward the room. Wondering idly why Drago didn't want him in, Manton followed Nestor.

It was a small salon, with a round table that held a bottle and glasses and a pack of sealed cards on its felt-covered top. Drago let Nestor break the seal, and gave him the deal. One school of gamblers played the cards, but Manton had always played the men, and now he leaned back to study them one by one.

Drago — percentage house man — Manton had known for a long time: excitable, not good at hiding his hand, but clever enough with the pasteboards. To Manton's left sat Ches Harrow, skinny and dissipated in a soiled flannel shirt and leather leggings without any fringe, his six-gun the only well-kept thing about him. Some along the river said he worked for the Big Three; others held he freelanced his skill with a gun. Bart Nestor, big and awkward and likable. Manton would have spotted him for a sucker but for the way he dealt. His callused fingers turned the cards into dancing light. The fourth man, between Drago and Manton, was a tall, cadaverous gent in a garish, purple fustian, and Manton had never seen him before.

"I'll take one."

"Open?"

"With a hundred."

It was the old ritual, and Manton was hardly listening. He played close to his vest, still studying the men, staying when he drew one queen to the pair in his hand. Drago took the pot with a flush, and the deal passed on to him. He shuffled and dealt with a professional carelessness. His instant's delay over certain cards might have missed men like Nestor or Harrow. It didn't miss Manton. When he picked up his cards, he ran a super-sensitive little finger along their bottoms. He had one king, and, sure enough, it bore two distinct cuts from Drago's thumb nail. One cut for aces, two for kings, three for queens — that was the way they were tabbed. But it was the oldest dodge, used only in tinhorn river dives. Diamond Hall — and all of Omaha, for that matter — was owned by the Big Three: Georges Arvada and Harry Wilkes and Diamond Jack. Manton couldn't feature them using such a small-time phony as thumbnail tabs to get what few pennies this game was worth.

With those marked cards in circulation,

Drago would know who held what, and Manton passed on his first draw. He wasn't surprised when Nestor took the pot with two pair. That was the come-on.

The man in the purple fustian took next deal. Patently he was a gambler of the first water, and should have felt those nail marks right away. He gave no sign. It puzzled Manton; he looked from Drago to the man in the fustian. Were they in this together?

As Manton took his cards, he bent his elbow imperceptibly to loosen the Derringer in its spring clip up his coat sleeve. Something was building, and he didn't like it. He had a pair of queens and three small spots. On the first draw he discarded two and drew in a duo of kings.

"Staying, Manton?"

Two pair were good enough; he shoved in his blues. "Staying and raising. One hundred."

"Harrow?" answered the man in the fustian.

"Gimme two."

The dealer flipped over a pair. "Staying?"

"Yeah, yeah . . . raising it another hundred."

Manton only half heard. He was asking himself what the hell they were doing. Ches Harrow had turned to watch Nestor.

14

Drago's bloodshot eyes, too, were centered on the bearded young man with a peculiar intensity. And, after shooting a sardonic glance at Manton, the man in the purple coat focused on Nestor. His voice sounded tighter, somehow, when he asked him: "Draw?"

"Two," grinned Nestor, in that engaging way. "Make 'em good."

Perspiration gleamed on Drago's sallow forehead. Harrow held his cards in his left hand. His right lay on the edge of the table, not six inches above the butt of his gun. From the first, it had been obvious that Nestor was card-wise. Manton wasn't surprised when he saw the emigrant's callused little finger slip under the bottom of the two cards he had just drawn. The smile on Nestor's face disappeared. Manton crooked his arm a little more. Harrow's fingers slid off the table till just their tips rested on the edge. Then Nestor laid his hand down with a slapping sound that was loud in the sudden hush.

"Tabbed!" he roared. "You've tabbed these cards. You bunch of tinhorn poker faces thought you could play me for a sucker, and you've marked these pasteboards."

Drago shoved his chair back and stood

up, but somehow the anger in his face wasn't convincing to Manton; his voice didn't sound vehement enough.

"You better back those words!" he shouted.

Red with anger, Nestor surged up, straddling his chair, shouting: "Damned right, I'll back 'em."

It all happened before he finished yelling. The man in the fustian let his cards flutter into his lap, and Nestor's clumsy draw would never match the swift, smooth way his hand slipped beneath that purple coat. At the same instant, Harrow's right hand slid off the table, and his draw was professional, too, and it left Nestor facing two men who would have their guns out long before he did.

But Manton had spotted it coming, and all he had to do was straighten his bent arm with a jerk. The Derringer jumped from its spring clip and hit his palm and bellowed like a cannon. Harrow's chair tilted beneath him as he took the .51 slug and went over backward with a sick cry, dropping his six-gun with the hammer only half eared back. That hammer dropped as the gun left his hand, and the slug it knocked out went into the floor. Manton was already turned in his seat.

"I've got another load in this cutter," he said flatly. "Want it?"

The man in the purple fustian had been standing as he drew, and his knees were still bent — his hand only part way out of the coat with the gleaming butt of a gun showing between his fingers. He forced that sardonic smile, then let the gun slide back in, and sat down.

Drago's turning motion toward Manton might have been to take care of the big, river gambler, but it was the slowest move of all, and it was far too late He stood there, unable to hide the baffled anger in his dull eyes. Nestor's gun wasn't out of its holster yet, and his face was just beginning to turn pale as he realized what Manton had saved him from.

"If we want to get out of here at all," Manton told him, "it had better be now."

There was a growing sound of voices outside, and someone began pounding on the flimsy door. Manton opened it, shoved Nestor out ahead of him, and backed out so the crowd couldn't see how he held that Derringer on Drago and the other man. He shut the door quickly on Drago and the other, shoving the crowd away.

"Nothing to get excited about," he said calmly. Then he turned to a bouncer with a

17

cauliflower ear and a checked vest that didn't fit his bulging shoulders. "Get in front of this door and don't let anybody in or out. I'm going for the doc and the sheriff."

Used to obeying orders, the man automatically shoved through the press to the door. Nestor began elbowing wildly to get free of the shifting knot of men, and Manton caught Nestor's arm, his voice a tense mutter. "Bolt now and you'll have every bouncer in the place on our necks before we reach the stairs."

Gripping Nestor by the elbow, Manton moved through the crowd in a walk just swift enough to look like a man going for the doctor, yet not fast enough to look like a man running away. They were moving by the roulette table when Drago's muffled voice came from inside the room.

The bouncer opened the door slightly. "Nobody gets in or out. That's orders."

"Whose orders?" raged Drago.

"That gent in the claw hammer," the bouncer said.

Manton still kept Nestor to a walk. They were on the first step, the second. . . .

"You fool," came Drago's yell. "That's the guy who shot Harrow. Harrow's been killed, damn you, and that guy in the claw hammer did it. Let me out. Grab him!"

"Now," snapped Manton.

They took the red-carpeted stairway three steps at a time and hit the bottom floor running. A startled bouncer made a half-hearted attempt to intercept Manton. The gambler hit him in the face, and he fell away, grunting. The crowd around the billiard tables shifted into Nestor's way. The big youth plowed through them, Manton in his wake. The man with the cauliflower ear came into view on the stairs, Drago behind.

"Stop that guy!" screamed the dealer. "He shot Harrow. That guy in the claw hammer. Ed Manton."

But Nestor was already through the batwings, taking one with him. Manton followed him out onto the plank walk. They turned right, running past the Douglas House on the corner, crossing the muddy street. The lights of the Apex Saloon reeled by. Behind came excited shouts, a shot, the pound of feet. Manton turned the next corner, ran a few feet to the door of a cheap hotel, shoved Nestor in. The night clerk jumped erect from behind the counter, blinking sleep-fogged eyes.

"Back way out?" snapped Manton.

Dazedly the man motioned toward a rear door. The gambler cut through it, rounded the few rickety dining tables, shoved through a swinging door at the back end. It was another dark room, apparently a kitchen. There was a clanging sound as Nestor bumped into a row of pots, cursing. Then they were out in a back alley, standing there a moment, breathing hard.

"You saved my life good and proper," said Nestor. "Though I can't see why. Seems to me you'd have stuck with your own kind when it came to something like that."

"They're not my kind," said Manton. "I've been a free-lance all my life, bucking big houses like the Hall, dealers like Drago. It was natural I'd take your side, I guess. I did it without thinking. And I never did like cold-deckers anyway. I can't understand, though, why they should play you for a sucker that way. Diamond Hall is too big a layout to use such small-time tabs as thumb-nail marks. It almost looked like they wanted you to spot 'em, wanted you to. . . ."

"Whatever they were up to," broke in Nestor, "it leaves you in a spot. I've been through Omaha three times before, taking the Oregon Trail, and I know what kind of a hold the Big Three have on the town. If Harrow was working for them, they won't let this pass. They'll be looking for you. A man doesn't stay alive long when they're looking for him . . . so I hear."

Manton knew Nestor was right. Arvada and Wilkes and Diamond Jack kept their grip on Omaha secure by liquidating anyone who bucked them, large or small. And now Manton had bucked them.

"Where'll you head?" asked Nestor. "You can't stay here."

Manton shrugged. What did it matter where he went? He felt nothing but the old, jaded indifference to the trail before him. Ten years ago he would have looked forward with a certain youthful eagerness to the next town up the river. But now he was thirty, and the next town would be the same as a hundred towns behind him. The smoky saloons, the gamblers with their dead faces and dead bodies and dead souls — like him — following a trail that led nowhere, unable to quit because the cards were in their blood.

"You couldn't leave Omaha by the river," said Nestor. "The Big Three'll have the boats watched. Why not come with me, Manton? I'm boss of a wagon train pulling out for Oregon tomorrow. Why not come along?"

"What's your cut?" Manton asked.

"My cut?" Nestor flushed angrily. "I don't get any. You saved my life, that's all, and I'm grateful. I was just trying to pay you back a little."

"I've been told those boom towns along the trail are a regular paradise for the knights of the green cloth," mused Manton, apparently not even listening to Nestor. "I guess it's as good a direction as any. Where are your wagons?"

They had parked just east of the sawmill, and their big orangewood wheels still dripped viscid river mud from the Lone Tree Ferry landing at the other end of Davenport Street. There were huge Pennsylvanias worth fifteen hundred dollars new, and carrying a pay load of four and a half tons; swagger-boxed Pittsburghs with their red and yellow paint already faded and peeling, three or four spans of heavy mules standing hipshot in battered traces. Nestor stopped by the lead wagon, a high-sided Conestoga. He looked at it proudly, slapped a wheel.

"This is my outfit. Best wagon out of Pittsburgh. I've been in Oregon before . . . know what it takes. New iron axles with rings in the ends to hitch up extra teams when we get bogged down, white oak bed, and extra long stakes to loosen the box when we ford the rivers. If anybody gets there, it'll be me."

He grinned like a kid with a new toy, and, once again, Manton realized how much youth that black beard hid. But that very youth was Nestor's charm. The gambler couldn't remember when he'd been drawn so strongly to anyone, and it struck him suddenly how long he had been traveling alone.

At the sound of Nestor's voice, a woman had come around the wagon, skirting the dropped tailgate. Manton shifted his indifferent gaze, and then the indifference slipped away. He stared.

His world for so long had been one of guile and masks and subterfuge. The women he had known always hid something behind their false smiles, always made their talk ambiguous. But this woman's deep, blue eyes would never know how to narrow with guile. Her young, red lips would always mean what they said, would hide nothing behind their frank smile. Her face bore none of the paint Manton had become used to on women. Her thick, fair hair was done up in two braids that hung to either side of cheeks colored and glowing with an outdoors health unfamiliar to the gambler.

She looked at him frankly.

"Leah, my sister," said Nestor. "Leah . . . Mister Manton."

She nodded to Manton, and he liked the

23

way her sunburned braids bobbed about the shoulders of her starched white crinoline. She turned to Barton Nestor.

"You got the stock, didn't you, Bart?"

He flushed and looked down at the ground, shuffling his great, black, square-toed boots in the muddy wheel ruts.

The woman's eyes suddenly glistened with tears. "Bart, you didn't gamble that money away? You know you spent too much on the wagon and left us our old team . . . you know they won't last us across to Oregon. Bart, you didn't . . . ?"

"I thought I could run it up and get some spare animals besides," he mumbled. "I'm sorry, Leah."

"You and your gambling," she said, choking. Then she glanced at Manton, face flaming, voice caustic. "Bart, I suppose you lost more than you had, and Mister Manton came along to collect the rest."

Manton felt himself flush under her obvious contempt, and it surprised him. He hadn't done that in years.

Barton Nestor looked up. "Matter of fact, Leah, you've got Manton all wrong. He saved my life. They marked the deck on me and had me all staked out for a cooling on both sides."

She turned from Manton, shoulders sagging hopelessly. Then she stumbled toward the rear of the wagon, fighting her tears with clenched fists. Bolsters creaked, and a moment later her muffled sobs came from inside. Nestor put out a long arm and leaned against the high box, grumbling: "Cuss me and my card fever. Every time we get some money saved, I try to run it up higher with the pasteboards. I guess it's in my blood . . . I just can't resist it."

Manton's gray eyes went to the broad-shouldered boy, knowing only too well what he meant. Fever it was, and, once a man was in deep enough, he was lost.

Nestor looked past Manton then, and the gambler could hear the slap of hoofs in the muddy street behind. He turned as the trio of riders hauled their mounts to a stop beside him. The lead horsebacker forked a huge, jugheaded mare, sitting the plain, black saddle with appalling ease for such a big, thick-torsoed man. His long, dark tail coat hung in expensive-cut lines from heavy shoulders, reaching the knees of his black trousers. Beneath a flat-crowned soft brim, his smile showed white teeth in a swarthy face. In the moonlight, it took Manton that moment to recognize him. Georges Arvada and Harry Wilkes and Diamond Jack were the Big Three. This was Georges Arvada.

☞ Two

" 'Evening, Manton," said Arvada softly. "I hear you had a little shooting scrape at the Hall."

Manton's arm crooked slightly to loosen his hide-out.

Arvada had been on the river a long time. He didn't miss the slight movement. "I was looking for the wagon boss," he said.

Nestor moved forward. He knew of the Big Three but, apparently, had never seen Arvada, for there was no sign of recognition on his face. "I'm the boss," he said.

"I've got four wagons and a double crew for Oregon," grinned Arvada. "I'd like to join your train."

"That's up to the people," said Nestor. "Though, as far as I'm concerned, there aren't any objections. The more wagons, the safer it is. You understand the rules, of course."

Arvada nodded. "Sure, we do our share of the work and the hunting and scouting. . . ."

"Wait a minute, Arvada," said Manton. "What are you trying to pull?"

Arvada's grin broadened. "You mean the business at Diamond Hall, I take it. Whatever happened there doesn't concern me, Manton. I've sold out. Omaha's getting too settled for me. The Big Three is now the Big Two, and whatever Harry and Diamond Jack want done about you, they'll have to do it themselves."

Manton reserved his opinion about that, and he still kept his arm bent a little. Arvada swung off his jughead with a lithe grace that was surprising in such a heavy-set man. But then he had always moved that way. It came from savate. The name sounded Spanish — Arvada — but he was really a Creole from New Orleans who had made his stake as a *voyageur,* a riverman, working the big Mackinaw boats down the Missouri. Among the *voyageurs* none had equaled Georges Arvada at savate, the Canuck way of fighting with the feet. His fame had reached from New Orleans to the British Territories, and more than one man had died beneath his cruel, pounding boots. A big part of savate consisted of juggling the weight from one leg to another so that one foot was always free to kick. It took skill and talent, and, if a man did it enough, he began to walk that way all the time, shifting his weight from side to side in an oddly graceful, calculating way, like a dancing master who could never forget his two-step.

But Arvada's days on the river were far behind him. He and Harry Wilkes and Diamond Jack had pooled their resources and built Diamond Hall, and had taken over Omaha. The rich, soft living of the past few years had thickened Arvada about the waist, had put a heaviness into his face. It surprised Manton that he should retain that old, smooth movement that came to a man who had fought savate on the wild Missouri.

The Creole turned to one of the men sitting a shaggy nag behind him. "Butler, go back and tell those 'skinners they can swing the wagons in line."

As Butler turned his horse, the third man dismounted. He was tall and lean, with shiny black hair cut like a Kansa Indian's, falling straight down the back of his neck from beneath a center-creased Stetson. His foxed California pants were stuck into fancy-topped Justins, and the way his pair of Paterson Colts were strapped about his supple hips left no question as to his profession.

It came to Manton suddenly . . . the batwing doors of Diamond Hall swinging shut behind him . . . the percentage men nibbling the free lunch . . . and the man in foxed California pants standing by the cuspidor. That man spoke suddenly, voice thick with a drink. "This the boy who nailed Harrow, Georgie?"

Georges Arvada nodded. "Yeah, Ringo. Ed Manton."

Any other man with as much liquor in him as Ringo carried would have been flat on his face in the mud and out cold long ago. Yet, somehow, Ringo moved forward, maintaining his equilibrium with solemn, drunken dignity, until his flushed face was within a foot of Manton's, drink-fogged eyes staring straight into the gambler's. Arvada was watching Ringo closely, waiting for something.

"Harrow was a good man," mumbled the drunk, his head moving closer to Manton as he swayed forward. "Yeah, good man. How'd a tinhorn like you ever edge him out?" He reached out with his pale, slim hands and pawed at Manton, frisking him, voice raising till it was almost shrill. "Or maybe you didn't draw with him . . . maybe you got a hide-out, a stinking little hide-out. . . ."

"Take your hands off me."

It must have been the utterly cold, toneless way Manton said it. Ringo took a surprised step backward, looking blankly at the gambler for a moment. Then the flush in his

29

face darkened, and he swayed forward precariously. He tried to say something, but for a moment his lips worked whitely without any sound coming out. His right hand began twitching above the silver-inlaid handle of his Paterson, and Manton knew what would happen in the next instant. He had expected it. What else should Arvada have come for? That tale about selling out was a little transparent, even for the Creole. Manton had never been a gun artist, and he doubted that he could meet Ringo's draw with his Derringer. He set himself.

Then Arvada stepped in front of Ringo. "Take it easy, Johnny boy. Mister Manton's already killed one man tonight. He must be tired."

It caught Manton off guard, but the old control kept his surprise from showing, and he regarded the Creole with eyes a dull, indifferent gray behind their narrowed lids, and he was wondering — *What kind of cards, Arvada, just what kind of cards are you holding at this table?*

Then he turned his back on the both of them. "Where do I sleep, Nestor?"

They got started before sunup next morning. Manton woke stiff and cold in the buffalo robe Nestor had given him, lying beneath the bed of the big Conestoga, listening for a moment to the crack of whips, the complaining bawl of cattle. Beside the next wagon, a bullwhacker was driving his oxen around in a circle to warm them, the big center chain dragging between each span, huge links clanking across the short prairie grass and through the muddy ruts leading from the city. Farther on, a red-shirted muleskinner was cursing his long-eared animals into their trees.

Manton rolled from beneath the Conestoga finally, walked to the campfires in the middle of the corral. The drivers had already eaten; there were a few emigrants in homespun still gulping down bitter, black coffee. Leah Nestor gave Manton some bacon and sourdough.

Bart Nestor came over a few minutes later, long blacksnake coiled in his callused hand. "How about helping me with the mules, gambler?" he grinned. "If you don't know how, you might's well start learning. Everybody lends a hand."

Manton went with him, stopping to wipe the grease from the bacon off his hands in the shortgrass. They passed a thick-tired Pittsburgh where two men were struggling vainly to lever a huge packing box over the tailgate into the bed. A gigantic teamster lumbered over from the next wagon, muttered something that Manton couldn't hear. The pair of men let go the box, stepped back. The other stopped, got his great hands beneath the edges. When he lifted, there was no apparent effort, and the box slid into the wagon easily. Nestor saw Manton watching.

"That's Mackinaw Williams," he volunteered. "Comes from Arkansas. I've seen a lot of strong men, but he tops 'em all. Must be six six and three hundred pounds on the hoof, and he's even stronger than he looks."

"Which introduces me," said Manton, "to another of my traveling companions."

Nestor's grin faded. "You aren't exactly happy about this trip, are you, Manton?"

Manton didn't answer, and moved on to Nestor's outfit. It was a hot, dusty, maddening job, harnessing the mules. He hadn't worked with traces and bit chains and hames that way since he was a kid, and his hands, usually so deft and skillful, turned into clumsy things that refused to do his bidding. Nestor put his heart into it, swearing happily at the mules, kicking at them and laughing at their outraged brays. Manton worked silently, sweat dribbling out of his light hair into his eyes, salty, stinging.

As wagon boss, Nestor had to be all up

and down the line on his short-coupled roan, and Leah Nestor drove their wagon. Manton sat up beside her on the high box seat, behind the dust-caked, bobbing rumps of the mules.

The buffalo grass west of Omaha was green with spring, and there was a fresh morning dampness in the air. The trail passed near the broad, yellow Platte most of the time, and, when a meadowlark called from the bright fringe of cottonwoods, Manton realized how long it had been since he had heard a bird sing.

"You're a strange man, Mister Manton."

The woman's voice brought him out of his reverie, and he turned to her. Morning sun caught on her bright yellow hair, and the sparkle in her eyes bothered him, somehow.

"You're so utterly indifferent," she said, turning to flick her light whip expertly at an off-wheeler. "So cold and detached, and . . . well, almost tired of living. Were you always that way?"

No, he thought, *not always.* He shrugged his shoulders and spoke of something else, because there was no use in talking about what he had once been, or what he was now. "Your brother said he'd been over the Oregon Trail before."

She accepted the change of subject gracefully. "Yes, but this is the last time. The Homestead Law went into effect a year ago, and Bart filed on some land in Grande Ronde Valley on his last trip. Some others filed with him . . . an old scout named Owhee, Mackinaw Williams, Sol Lewis. They came back to get their families. Our group was the first to file in that valley, and we own almost all the land in it."

"Seems to me I've heard Grande Ronde is quite a choice spot."

"Oh, yes," she smiled. "Bart says it's a gold mine. The trail goes right through the center of the valley, and with more emigrants passing through every year the people who build a town there stand to make a fortune. Only yesterday, someone tried to buy Bart's claim . . . a Colonel Something-Or-Other. But Bart wouldn't sell. We've been looking forward to it for so long. Our folks died and left us the farm back in Iowa, but it was heavily mortgaged, and there were so many bad years. We had to let it go. Now we'll have new land, and a new house, even a new town. . . ."

She trailed off, and he could see the shine in her eyes. He wondered what it would be like to look forward to something like that, to dream of it, plan it, fight for it like these people were.

The mules plodded on. The dust rose in plumes that hung yellow over the creaking, swaying wagons, and the monotony of sound and movement had an hypnotic effect that caused Manton to doze off with the sweet smell of spring in his nostrils.

It was a time for buffalo calves to drop, and for the wallows to be ringed with the shedding cows and bulls, and for herds to be crossing the trail. The wagons passed Fremont, and Clarks, and the Grand Pawnee burial ground, and on the third day Nestor woke Manton up before the teamsters had begun to stir.

"Bunch of us are going to scout ahead for buffalo," he said. "I'll loan you my sorrel and a gun if you want to come. Better'n sitting on the cussed wagon all day long."

Nestor had a big White River saddle for the sorrel, double-rigged, heavy. It had been a long time since Manton had ridden. He was awkward with the cinches, and it made the horse distrustful from the first. Nestor got a big muzzle-loading Springfield from the wagon, along with a horn of powder and some balls.

"Keep the powder loose in your pocket," he explained. "You'll have to shoot at the running bulls. Guess at the amount you need and dump it in by hand when you're near enough. Wet the ball so it'll stick to the powder and won't roll out the barrel if you have to shoot downward."

There were half a dozen men sitting their mounts in the dim morning light outside the corralled wagons. Among them was the old scout, Owhee, dressed in greasy buckskins and a shaggy, wolfskin hat. He forked a split-ear buffalo pony bareback, knees thrust into the hair rope around its barrel. It was still not light enough to distinguish features, but Manton could see the dim blur of the men's faces turn toward him as he rode up.

"I told you no tenderfeet this fust time, Nestor," said Owhee, bulging a gnarled cheek out with his chewing tobacco and speaking in a high, cracked voice. "What good'll a tail-coat gambler do? We ain't out for the sport. The train needs meat."

Close up like that, Manton could see the silver mounting gleaming dully on the saddle of a piebald, could see the long, lean figure swaying back and forth in that saddle as if blown by a light breeze. Johnny Ringo.

"Manton goes," said Nestor.

Georges Arvada, too, towered beside Ringo on his huge mare, holding that easy seat. His face, like all the others, was a mere blur, but it was turned toward Manton, and the gambler could feel those flashing black eyes on him, speculative. Ringo laughed nastily.

"They gave him a gun, Owhee, can't you see?" he said. "He isn't any tenderfoot, now. He's a regular buff'lar hunter."

Owhee spat and wheeled his split-ear, cursing in a disgusted way. Still laughing, Ringo jammed a brutal, silver-plated spur into his piebald and took out after the scout. Arvada followed, and the others. Some of them ignored Manton as they passed him; one or two still looked at him with a vague hostility. He kicked the sorrel into motion. What the hell? He didn't care what Arvada and Ringo thought, and he hadn't expected the others to accept him, anyway. He just wasn't their kind.

They found a wallow where a small herd was browsing, shortly before noon, and shot half a dozen of the shaggy bulls before the rest stampeded. Brought by some morbid instinct of death, coyotes formed a ring around the hunters where they were butchering the carcasses, and, farther out, the dark shapes of loafer wolves appeared like somber shadows on the rolling plain. Above, on silent, waiting wings, swung black buzzards. It oppressed Manton, and he was glad when they'd butchered all the meat the horses could carry. In his saddlebags were thick steaks, and across the withers of the sorrel hung strips of *doupille,* back fat that ran all the way from hump to hocks on a bull.

Nestor led back toward the trail, Manton beside him, and they were the first to see the man ahead, lying in a shadowed roll of prairie, horse standing hipshot a few yards away, cropping half-heartedly at some cream-colored soapweed. His long legs in their fringed, buckskin leggings were twisted in an awkward position as if he had fallen that way from his mount, and, as Manton approached, he could see the dark stain spreading from the puckered bullet hole in the gray serge vest. The man's dish chin bore a week's growth of blond beard, and his eyebrows and long hair were the same bleached color against the reddish brown of his haggard, young face. Manton swung down, knelt, and put an ear to his chest.

"He's still breathing," he said finally, slipping an arm under the sunburned head. "Take that meat off the sorrel, will you, Nestor? . . . and I'll put him aboard."

"No sense in wasting good meat on *him,*" said Arvada from behind. "That's Vern Beatrie."

Nestor got off his horse and bent over the man. "Lord, is that Beatrie? He's just a kid, isn't he?"

"Dirtiest killer on the frontier," said Arvada. "Got more notches on his gun than any other ten trigger artists. I say we leave him out here for the buzzards."

Manton rose and turned to face Arvada. "He's still alive, and I wouldn't leave any man out here for the buzzards, Arvada . . . not even you."

Arvada's swarthy face turned a dull red, and he leaned forward in his saddle, eyes flashing. "I stopped Johnny Ringo the other night because I didn't want any trouble our first evening in camp, Manton. But you seem bent on starting something. Maybe we should leave you out here for the buzzards, too."

Nestor stepped forward. "Now wait a minute, Arvada. . . ."

"Keep out of this, Nestor," broke in the Creole harshly. "You know as well as I do we'd be fools to save a killer like Beatrie. He'd likely turn around and put a slug through our backs as soon as we'd nursed him well."

Manton stepped to his sorrel, pulling the buffalo meat off, dropping it on the ground. Then he bent down and lifted Beatrie's shoulders up, slipped his arm under the man, got his own broad shoulder beneath him. There was a lot of weight in Beatrie's lanky, broad-shouldered body. Manton was breathing harder when he finally got him across his horse. Then he heard the sibilant scrape of leather leggings sliding out of a saddle. When he turned around, Johnny Ringo was standing by his piebald.

"Take him off that horse, Manton," he said thickly.

Arvada's flushed face was suddenly split by his flat-lipped, white-toothed smile, and he kneed his jughead out of the way. The other riders eased away, and, looking at their faces, Manton saw that he stood alone. Owhee spat, grunted: "Better do it, gambler. Like Arvada says, we don't want no killer in our midst."

Arvada was still grinning, the anger gone from his eyes because he still held all the aces. "Ringo's a wizard with those Patersons when he's swacked, Manton, and right now he's carrying more liquor than the whole bunch of us could hold put together."

"It would seem that was always the case," said Manton.

Ringo was swaying back and forth like a young willow in a high wind. His right hand began twitching above his gun, and his voice

40

took on that shrill, almost hysterical note. "Take him off that horse, Manton, damn you, take him off that horse . . . !"

Manton's craggy face remained set in a cold, indifferent mask that didn't betray his blinding move. He was suddenly a blurred figure in a flapping, black claw hammer, slamming forward to meet Ringo with a stunning force. The gunman's right hand was still twitching above his Paterson as Manton hit him, and he staggered backward with a surprised cry.

One of Manton's big fists was already gripping the lapels of Ringo's vest. The other slapped Ringo's face with a loud crack. Holding him up that way, Manton continued to slap the man, rocking his black head back and forth with stunning blows.

Ringo's breath was knocked from him with each slap, coming as a series of involuntary wheezes. He forgot all about drawing. He hit at Manton with futile fists. He kicked vainly with those fancy-topped Justins. A bitter curse burst from his white, writhing lips.

Then Manton straightened his arm and let go of the vest, and Ringo went onto his back, dust popping up from beneath him, curses cut off by a sick, jarred grunt. Manton took a step and stood over him, waiting coldly for him to rise.

Face beet red from the slaps, breath coming in uncontrollable gusts, Ringo struggled to his feet. Before he was quite erect, Manton took another step, forcing the gunman to stumble backward to keep from being knocked over again. Manton kept on going, shoving the man on back, off balance, until he slammed into the side of his piebald and couldn't go any farther. Then Manton stood there, his utterly cold face not a foot from Ringo's.

Beaten, panting, Ringo sagged weakly against his mount's sweaty flank. He met Manton's flat, gray stare for an instant, then his bloodshot eyes flickered from side to side, going helplessly to Arvada.

"Well, Ringo . . . ?" said Manton in that toneless way.

Ringo drew a choked breath. His hand began to twitch again, then stopped. Manton waited for another long moment, then for the second time turned his back on the man, and walked to his sorrel. Arvada sat his jughead quietly, and for a moment his eyes rested on Manton with a certain new respect. Then he looked at Ringo, and the twist that came into his mouth might have been contempt.

It was almost night, now, and they headed

toward the trail swiftly, Manton carrying Beatrie across the withers of his horse. Nestor rode beside him, looking from time to time at the gambler, puzzled.

"You were taking a mighty big chance, Manton," he said. "You aren't any short gun artist, and that Ringo's got about the itchiest finger on the frontier."

"Nestor," said Manton, "there are two kinds of gamblers. Those that play the cards, and those that play the man. Me, I've always played the man. Peg him, and what kind he is, and you've got the best odds any gambler could expect. I figure the reason Ringo keeps himself swacked all the time is that he'd be yellow if he was sober . . . he wouldn't be worth a plugged nickel with those guns. You can slap a lot of liquor out of a man that way."

"Maybe you're right," said Nestor. "Maybe he does use red-eye for guts. But I still think you were taking a mighty big chance. Supposing you hadn't knocked him as sober as you did. I don't think I'd back even your Derringer against those Patersons of his."

Manton bent his right arm, jerked it straight, and nothing came out. "I left the Derringer back in the wagon. Figured it would get in the way on a buffalo hunt."

🐃 Three

Lonetree was behind them now, and Grand Island, and Plum Creek. Leah had taken Vern Beatrie into her wagon and nursed him without any questions asked, and Manton admired her for that.

Wood River was a group of log houses around a stockade that was used as a dépôt for the Great Western Stage, and the night the wagons corralled just west of the settlement Beatrie got out of the Conestoga to eat with the others for the first time.

When the meal was over, most of the men and women gathered around the big center fire for a square dance. Manton and Beatrie sat against a wagon wheel outside the circle of light, listening to the scraping fiddle, the blurred talk. Manton rolled two wheat-straw cigarettes, lighting them from the coals of a smaller fire.

Beatrie accepted one, grinning at him. "You aren't a very curious cuss, are you, Manton?"

The gambler turned to him. "Not very. Why?"

Beatrie studied the glowing end of his cigarette. "You and the woman are just about the only ones who haven't been prying as to what I was doing out there on the prairie with a slug through my brisket. I like you for that, Manton."

Manton shrugged. "It was easy enough to draw conclusions."

Beatrie's laugh was harsh. "I had a run-in with an *hombre* in Omaha. He wasn't as quick with an iron as he thought. But the citizens weren't willing to let it go at that. Posse chased me out of town. I outrode 'em up there north of the Platte, but not before one of 'em had put my name on that bullet. Vern Beatrie . . . it said, right through my hump ribs."

Laughter rose from the milling crowd, and the fiddle scraped on. Beatrie took a final puff, ground his smoke into the grass.

"That gal," he grunted. "Leah Nestor. She takes a right big interest in you. Seemed to figure I was your kind, thought maybe I'd understand you. Asked me the other day what made you so damned indifferent to everything."

"Did you tell her?" Manton asked dryly.

Beatrie laughed. "Now I'm prying, ain't I? But I did tell her, because I am sort of your kind, and I know. My dad was a gambler, and I've seen enough others. Fascinating, when you first step in. Big money, painted women, cards that get their hold on you and won't let go. But always the time comes when you want to quit . . . and you suddenly find you can't. And after a while you get jaded, like a wind-blown horse, following a trail because it's the only one you can follow. That's my trail, too, Manton, and there's only one end to it. Sometimes I think I'd give my soul to find another. But as I get further along, those times get fewer and farther in between, and mostly I don't give a damn."

Manton's gray eyes were barely perceptible behind his narrowed lids, looking emptily toward the emigrants on the other side of the corral. It almost hurt, the way Beatrie had struck home. The past few years especially — that growing sense of the utter, hollow, uselessness of his life. And as Beatrie said, the further along the trail you got, the fewer and farther between were those brief moments when you'd give your soul to find another way. And finally they stopped, and you just didn't give a damn about anything.

"Why'd you pick me up out there on the prairie, Manton?" asked Beatrie suddenly. "You knew it would mean bucking Arvada and that swacked gun artist of his."

"I don't know exactly," said Manton. "Like you say, maybe you're my kind, in a way. Maybe that was it. Or maybe I was just getting tired of Ringo's little act."

"You're a pretty sizable man," said Beatrie in a musing way. "Looks like you were built for farming or something . . . something better than stud or draw or faro, than sitting at a table and getting soft and fat on women and cards and liquor. Did you ever want something real bad, Manton?"

Manton's face went blank with memory. There had been a time when he'd wanted everything that way, when he'd surged forward to meet life eagerly. But that time had passed. It seemed these days there was nothing left to want.

"Maybe," said Beatrie, "you ain't so far gone as you think. There's a lot of fight left in you. You fought Ringo because you wanted to bring me in. There's other things to fight for . . . better things. The girl, for instance. Leah. Would you fight for her?"

Manton's head raised. "Funny, I never thought about her that way. . . ."

"Let's see your hands," said Beatrie.

Manton held out his hands, turning to the blond man. They were gambler's hands, long-fingered, pale, supple. Yet they were big hands, too, and they held a strength that hadn't been dissipated by slick decks and stacks of blues.

"I always said a gambler would make a gunman," murmured Beatrie. "He has the control over his hands, the split-second timing. And he's developed a poker face that wouldn't give away his draw in a million years. You won't be able to fight for that gal with a Derringer in this country, Manton. And don't think you're finished with Ringo, either. He might be yellow, when he's sober, and you might have knocked the liquor from him once. But he keeps himself full of joy juice twenty-four hours a day, and the next time you cross horns with him, you won't get close enough to slap him. You might have matched Ches Harrow with your Derringer, but he was small-time compared to Ringo. Trying to use your Derringer against Ringo's Patersons would be like bucking a royal handful of three spots. Suicide."

They passed Fort Kearny the next day, and camped outside Dobytown, two miles west of the fort. Manton was unhitching the mules alone when Leah came up by the off leader and stood there. He rose from unsnapping the big chains, and looked across the mule's dusty back into her blue eyes, dark with worry. Her face was close, and the blood thickened in his throat.

"Manton," she said, "Bart's going into Dobytown for some flour and side-bacon. You know him and cards. I want you to go along and see that he doesn't get into any trouble."

"I'll finish the mules first."

"No," she said. "Go now. I've been handling mules ever since I was old enough to lift a headstall."

Nestor had borrowed a buckboard, and Beatrie was sitting in the back, dangling his long legs over the edge. The gigantic Arkansas boy, Mackinaw Williams, was standing by the horses, and with him was Sol Lewis, a bold scarecrow of a man with a caustic twist to his thin-lipped mouth. Nestor sat in the spring seat, grinning at Manton as he came up.

"Your sis told me to go with you and keep your hands off the cards," said the gambler, swinging aboard.

"Suits me," said Nestor, then turned to Mackinaw and the other. "Well, climb in and let's get going."

Lewis hitched at his galluses, casting a disgruntled look at Manton. "I guess I won't go, after all, Bart. Got to water my cattle before the others muddy the shallows."

A shadow passed over Mackinaw's freckled face, and he turned to follow Lewis, muttering: "Me, too, Bart. My horse hasn't been rubbed down since we left the Mizzou."

Manton followed them with his eyes; and his voice had a bleak sound. "Looks like I'm not exactly popular around here."

"Forget it," said Nestor with a hurt frown. "Those cornhuskers wouldn't know a good man if he was thrown in their faces."

He lashed out with his buggy whip suddenly, and the team lurched forward. Manton grabbed the warped seat as the buckboard lurched into a roll.

It was one of the wildest places on the Oregon Trail, Dobytown. Drunken soldiers from Kearny zigzagged down the middle of the muddy, wheel-rutted street; souses and barflies lay in stupors beneath the high plank sidewalk, feet sticking out from under the edge; ration Indians squatted against the baseboards of the buildings, eyes dull with tanglefoot whiskey. There were a dozen saloons and gambling halls in one block, ranging from a big two-story affair with a five-piece orchestra to a mud-chinked log hovel that had but one kind of liquor to offer, and that served from a barrel by the door. Nestor halted the buckboard in front of the Naked Truth Saloon, looking up at the sign above its plank overhang. He grinned suddenly, began to read it aloud:

Having just opened a commodious ship for the sale of liquid refreshment, I embrace this opportunity of informing you that I have commenced the business of making drunkards, paupers, and beggars for the sober, industrious and respectable portion of the community to support. I shall deal in family spirits which will incite men to deeds of riot, robbery, and blood, and by so doing diminish the comfort, augment the expenses, and endanger the welfare of the community. I will undertake on short notice and for a small sum to prepare victims for the asylum, poor farm, prison, and gallows. I will furnish an article which will increase fatal accidents, multiply the number of distressing diseases, and render those which are harmless, incurable. I will deal in a commodity which will deprive some of life, many of reason, most of pros-

perity, and all of peace, which will cause fathers to become fiends, children, orphans, and wives, widows. Welcome one and all.

"There," laughed Beatrie, "is a man after my own heart."

"Let's go in and wet our whistle," said Nestor. "I haven't had a swig of honest to goodness rotgut for weeks."

There was a tinny piano going, but beneath its discordant clatter Manton could hear other sounds — the clink of a glass and, in a momentary lull, the muted slap of cards, someone bidding. He could feel it creeping into him, the old fascination. His fingers curled up as if holding a deck. It had been weeks since he had sat at a table. Suddenly his mouth clamped to a thin, hard line, and he spoke through his teeth.

"Come on, Bart, we're getting the flour."

The others followed slowly.

The sutler's store was down the street, near the corner. Beatrie stopped in front of it, turning to Nestor. "You get the stuff. We'll meet you here in about twenty minutes."

The bearded youth nodded.

"And stay clear of those saloons," said Manton.

Beatrie took Manton's arm, turned him

down the walk and around the corner into a dingy side street. Their boots made a hollow sound on the plank walk, then it came to an end, and they stepped off into the mud, quartering across the mucky wheel ruts to a battered little sod and log house.

"Where are we headed?" asked Manton.

Beatrie grinned secretively. "Jimmie Thompson's. He's known from the Mizzou to the Rockies."

The door was made of pin-oak boards, hung on leather hinges. Beatrie had to lift it before it would swing open. There was a short counter in the gloomy room. Manton could scarcely make out the rifles in a rack to one side. A light showed through a half-open door that led to a back room.

"Jimmie," called Beatrie.

There was the sound of a scraping chair, the pad of feet on sod floor. The light suddenly flooded the room, and a bent, old man in a slick, leather smock stood there, oil lamp held in one gnarled, brown hand above his white head. His voice was high, cracked.

"By gonies, if it ain't Vern Beatrie. Thought the law'd have you six feet under by now, sonny."

"They would," grinned Beatrie, "except for my friend here. We want a gun, Jimmie, a six-gun."

"Well, now," muttered the old man, setting down his lamp and reaching beneath the counter, "how's this?"

It was a big, white-handled weapon in a stiff, shiny holster. Beatrie drew the gun free, spun the cylinder, cocked, and pulled the trigger.

"Newest thing by Sam Colt, Vern," said Thompson. "Rebated cylinder, center-fire cartridges, all the fixin's."

"Looks like an Army holster," said Manton.

The ancient gunsmith turned his white head to the gambler, showing a few broken teeth in his grin. "Younker, I never ask too close where my guns come from. Doesn't pay to do that out here. Fact is, I don't seem to rec'lect the name of the gazabo what sold me this lead-pusher. Or maybe he didn't give me his name." He cackled, turned back to Beatrie.

The blond man laid down the big Colt with a metallic clang. "That is the stiffest thing I've ever palmed, Jimmie," he said disgustedly. "You know what kind of a gun I want. Dig out one of your old ones."

Thompson looked from Beatrie to Manton, then grinned in that sly, toothless way. "I see what you mean. Hold your team a minute, while I go to the back room."

When he disappeared through the door, Manton turned to Vern Beatrie. "What's wrong with the gun you have now?"

"Nothing's wrong with my gun," said Beatrie. "I told you that Derringer of yours wasn't any good in the country we're heading for, Manton. Ringo isn't the only reason. You need an iron with some range, and with six slugs instead of two. They don't sit around card tables out there, y'know."

Thompson was back. He laid another six-shooter on the counter, passing his hands across the worn, well-oiled holster in what amounted to a caress.

"Navy Colt," said the gunsmith, almost reverently. "Lawman sold it to me. Got it off Hair Trigger Allison when he cashed in his chips. You remember Allison, Beatrie."

Beatrie nodded, hefting the big, black-handled Navy. "Good man, Allison. He took two deputies with him when he went out. With this gun, too. I don't like a Thirty-Six as well as a Forty-Four, but it has the kind of workings you want, Manton. You can see why they called him Hair Trigger Allison."

He shoved it into Manton's hand. The gambler slipped his finger around the curved trigger, cocking the gun. He didn't think he put any pressure on that trigger at all, yet almost before the hammer was eared back the gun jumped in his hand. It startled him, and Beatrie laughed.

"A good man could do a helluva lot with that kind of iron. Allison did. He was known from here to Port La Vaca. Get him going on that thing and it wouldn't stop till it was empty. We'll take it, Jimmie. How much?"

"Reg'lar Navy's eighteen fifty," said Thompson. "Seein' this is Allison's iron, it'll be twenty-five even."

Beatrie started to dig in his pocket. Manton caught his arm, slipped out his own wallet. They bought some shells and punched the empty loops of the cartridge belt full of .36 caps and balls. Then Manton strapped it on, thonged it around his thigh. With the weight of it awkward against his leg, he bid the old gunsmith good night and went out into the dark street behind Beatrie.

The far-off pound of running feet and sporadic yells came to them from the main street. They rounded the corner and saw three men running from the sutler's store toward the Naked Truth, others coming toward the saloon from the east end of town. A man panted by Manton, and the gambler called to him.

"Shooting in the Naked Truth," the man answered over his shoulder. "Some pilgrim got daylight let through him good and proper."

Manton could see the buckboard standing in front of the saloon, empty. He felt a sudden catch in his throat, and broke into a run, heavy body shaking the boards beneath him every time his boots hit the walk. He was going fast when he came to the crowd milling outside the bat-wings of the saloon. He put his shoulder into them, momentum carrying him halfway through before their packed bodies halted him.

To the tune of angrily shifting feet and sudden, pained curses he elbowed his way on through. There was another crowd, a smaller one, around one of the rear card tables. Manton shoved through them, and then he was standing there, breathing hard, looking down at Barton Nestor.

The young, black-bearded wagonmaster was sitting alone at the round deal table, head on his arms, three growing stains of blood on the back of his tan hickory jacket where the bullets had come through. For a moment, Manton couldn't accept the boy's death. Nestor had been so young and eager for life, with his broad grin and his wild way of forking that roan, and his weakness for cards. The friendship between them had never been expressed in words, because they were men, and sentiment like that was an awkward thing. Yet, it had been there, growing stronger and deeper with each day that passed. Manton felt a strange, dull pain, as if something vital had been torn from his own body. He turned, voice husky and low.

"Who shot him?"

A bartender rubbed nervous hands on his soiled apron. "The card players all faded, naturally. Nobody else saw it very well. I think there was a gent with a purple fustian sitting in on the game."

Beatrie had shoved through and stood above Nestor, lifting his dead fingers off the cards. "Just couldn't resist one game, could he? And look at the hand he got."

Manton glanced at the card that lay beneath Nestor's callused fingers. It was an ace of spades. "Looks like somebody tabbed him for the play," said the gambler. "An ace of spades is a dead man's card in any game."

Four

The dusty hackberries around the Plum Creek trading station were back of them now, and the Fur Trading House at Gothenburg, with its buildings of red cedar logs. Ahead was North Platte where the trail forked — the California Trail going north to Fort Laramie, the Julesburg route turning south.

Manton had known how the woman would take the news of her brother's death. Her chin had raised a little, and her small brown hands had clenched, and she controlled her grief that way. But later, sleeping in the buffalo robe beneath the wagon box, Manton had heard her hopeless sobs from the bed above him. Bart Nestor had dreamed of building a house there in the green bowl of Grande Ronde, and his sister had dreamed with him, and now that dream had been smashed by a card player who left an ace of spades to mark the man he had killed.

They made camp at North Platte the next day, and after supper Manton asked Beatrie to take him down to the river and teach him how to use that Navy .36. The two men passed through the outspanned wagons and went by the cavvy, browsing in the short-grass outside. Beatrie grinned faintly.

"Seems like you're more anxious to use that gun now than I was to have you get it, Ed."

"I have a score to settle," said Manton. "And when it comes time, I want to settle it right. Bart Nestor wasn't killed by chance."

"But he was one of the most likable cusses I've known," said the blond man. "Everybody in the wagon train loved him like a brother. Why would anyone want to kill a guy like that?"

"Grande Ronde is a good reason," said Manton. "From what I hear, all the alternate routes of the Oregon Trail converge before they reach Grande Ronde . . . the California Trail, the Mormon, the Julesburg, the Lander Cut-off. That means more emigrants pass through Grande Ronde than any other given spot on the rest of the trail. You can see what would happen to a town built in that valley."

Beatrie whistled. "Never figured it that way. It'd be the biggest boom town west of the Missouri."

"The emigrants have been going on to the Willamette, but that valley's filling up, and they've suddenly realized what a choice bit of ground Grande Ronde is," said Manton. "Bart Nestor and his friends just about control the valley with their homesteads. They don't care much about building any boom town. They're farmers, and they got that land to farm. I imagine there are quite a few men who hate to see a place like that go to waste. There was a syndicate that offered to buy Bart's land. Maybe, when they found out they couldn't get it legally, they decided to try other ways."

Beatrie let that soak in. "But why just knock off Nestor? There are a half a dozen others here in the train with homesteads in the valley. Lewis, Mackinaw, even Owhee. And who's doing it?"

"I don't know why Nestor was the goat. And as to who's doing it . . . the bartender at the Naked Truth mentioned a gent in a purple fustian. Back at Diamond Hall there was a man wearing a purple fustian who sat in with two others to cold-deck Nestor. At the time, Ringo was in the lower lobby of the Hall. Arvada owns . . . or owned . . . a third interest in the Hall. If you add those things up, I don't know whether the answer you get will be true or not."

Manton could see well enough, now, why Drago had thumb-nailed those cards, why

61

he hadn't wanted Manton to sit in. The whole thing had been a set-up, built around Nestor's skill with the cards, and his hot temper. They marked the pasteboards for him to feel, and planted Harrow and the man in the purple fustian for what was sure to follow. And if Manton hadn't interfered, it would have been just another unfortunate fool killed in a card game, with no one guilty of anything more than self-defense.

Manton and Beatrie went through a motte of cottonwoods, greening with summer, and came out into the bottom-lands. A black and white lark flushed from some wild plum trees ahead of them, circling swiftly upward.

"Take off that coat," said Beatrie. "You can't have your tails getting mixed up with your hand when you dive."

Manton removed the claw hammer, folding it on the ground. Then they went to work. Beatrie showed him how to crouch and dive, how to grab the gun with his thumb hooked for the hammer so it would be cocked by the time it cleared the edge of the holster. He taught him how to fan with the heel of his hand, or with his thumb.

"I always said a gambler would make a good gunman," grinned Beatrie. "Palming an ace with four men watching takes just as much split-second timing as slapping for iron. And that poker face is a natural. Nobody'll ever spot your draw. You'll have Hair Trigger Allison turning over in his grave with shame. Now draw, any time you're ready."

Only then did Manton see why Beatrie was known as one of the most dangerous gunmen on the frontier. The gambler crouched and slapped at his Navy, yet it hadn't begun to leave leather when Beatrie's .44 was already above the rim of its holster. And Manton couldn't have sworn Beatrie's hand had moved.

"That's OK, Manton," laughed Beatrie. "I've been in the game a long time. Try again, and don't give yourself away by crouching before you begin to move your hand."

Yes, thought Manton, *and Ringo's been in the game a long time, too.* . . . . He set himself again and crouched and dove, and again Beatrie's gun came out long before he had even begun to pull his upward.

"You're dead," said Beatrie. "Like a stick of wood cracking in the middle. That crouch is to put spring in your draw. Dip with your knees until your iron is about halfway out, then spring back up. It helps jump your gun out. Now, try again."

Manton tried again, and again, and again. Sweat ran down the craggy lines of his sun-darkened face, turned his shirt soggy, leaked into his eyes, salty and stinging. But grimly he hung on, and there came one time when his gun was almost out before Beatrie's had cleared leather. Beatrie laughed in a pleased way, the teacher who had found one pupil in a million.

"Why did you ever take up the paste-boards anyway, Manton? You have more natural gun talent than. . . ."

He trailed off suddenly. Manton followed his glance as he turned toward the cotton-woods. Johnny Ringo stood there, holding his piebald with its silver-mounted saddle. His lips pulled flatly away from his teeth in a mirthless smile, and he swayed forward.

"Well, well," he said thickly, "Manton's gonna be a trigger artist now. When you learn which way to point the gun, tinhorn, come around. Yeah, come around. I'll show you a few things Beatrie never heard of before."

Laughing nastily, he led his horse between them and on down to the river.

Beatrie's face had taken on a tight look, and he couldn't quite keep the anger from his voice. "Seems to me I saw him water that horse about an hour ago. Must be a right thirsty critter."

★ ★ ★

Ringo had gone back to the wagons, and Manton was slipping on his coat, when the blue-grass swished and the woman topped the roll of land between them and the cottonwoods. Her face was flushed and glowing beneath her yellow hair, and her lips were parted, glistening. There had been other women in Manton's life, and more than once he thought he had loved. Looking at Leah now, he knew he hadn't. The emotion he had felt had been dull and cheap and false compared with what swept him now, at the sight of her standing there.

"You've got to come to the wagons quick," she said. "Arvada's crowd wants to take the California Trail, and they're bulling it through over the heads of the whole train. That route's been avoided the last two years because of the Indian raids. If we take it, there's a good chance we'll be wiped out."

"What good will I do?" asked Manton. "I haven't any voice."

"You have more than you realize," she said. "Bart's friends know what happened between you and Ringo. That puts you on their side. They need a leader, Ed. Since Bart's been . . . gone, they've split up and started quarreling among themselves. Arvada can push them around just as he pleases."

He stood there in the gathering darkness, looking away from her, his face expressionless. "I'm not your kind, Leah, not your people's kind. They'll never understand me, and they won't listen to a man they don't understand."

She caught him by the elbows, throwing her head back so she could look up at him, eyes wide and flashing anger. "Of course, they don't understand you, Ed Manton. You won't let them. You hide all your feelings behind that mask. You're our kind . . . you're flesh and blood. You're a big man, Ed, a strong one, meant for strong feelings. If you'd only show them those feelings, show them you're human . . . they'd follow you. Don't you see what it means to them . . . to me? They wanted those homesteads in Grande Ronde bad enough to work and sweat and fight and even die all the way from Missouri and Arkansas and Iowa. Haven't you ever wanted anything bad enough to suffer and sacrifice . . . to get good and mad and fight for? Haven't you?"

She was half sobbing when she finished, and tears were on her flushed cheeks. He could feel her trembling against him with the force of her emotion.

Beatrie had asked him the same thing, and he had the answer now. *Sure I want something bad enough to fight for,* he thought. *I want you, Leah.* The words were welling up in his throat, and for a moment he thought he could tell her.

"Leah . . . ," he began, "I. . . ."

Then, somehow, he couldn't go on. Her eyes watched him expectant, almost pleading. But for too many years he had suppressed all emotion, had cultivated that careful, cold control over himself, building a wall that cut him off from the rest of the world. And now he found he couldn't express the unfamiliar emotions that boiled up within him. His eyes were narrowed to hide the bitter sense of frustration he felt, and he heard his voice coming out in that old, flat, toneless way.

"I'll see what I can do, Leah."

He caught the disappointment in her big eyes, then was moving around her and over the rise of bottomland into the shadows of the cottonwoods. When he reached the wagons, he could see the crowd gathered on the far side of the corral, could catch the flash of a teamster's red wool shirt, the white blur of an upraised fist. And the bull voice of Clew Butler, Arvada's wagon boss, coming from the middle of the bunch.

Manton reached the fringe and grabbed a man's shoulder, shoving him aside. His other hand caught at a man's galluses and yanked him back. The next muleskinner turned. Seeing Manton, he suddenly elbowed his way aside, leaving the way clear, saying his name.

"Manton."

It was like an open sesame. More men turned, and, when they saw the gambler, they shoved each other to make a path leading into the center. It surprised Manton a little.

Arvada's muleskinners seemed to form the inner ranks, half a dozen thick-bellied, square-chested men with heavy beards, one of them holding a heavy breech-loader, the others packing short guns in a familiar way. Clew Butler must have stood over six feet in his red wool socks, with the strength of the bulls he drove showing in his long arms, thick and hairy beneath the rolled-up sleeves of his flannel shirt. Georges Arvada was standing beside him, facing the men, and Manton couldn't help admiring the compelling effect of his smooth voice.

"When Nestor died," he was telling the emigrants, "you chose Clew here because he was the only one among you who knew the country. He's been over the trail a dozen times, and if he says the California's the fork to take, it's up to you to abide by his decision."

Coming up the Missouri from Arkansas, the spring rains had shrunk Mackinaw Williams's cotton shirt so tight that the tremendous rolling bulge of his shoulder muscles kept splitting it across the back, and he had quit trying to keep it sewed up. His voice sounded above the shuffle of feet and sullen muttering like a grizzly's roar over the *churr* of red squirrels.

"Seems to me we didn't do no choosing. You and your crowd just sort of elected Butler yourselves, and with Nestor gone we couldn't get any organization to stop you with."

Arvada ignored him. "I'm telling you . . . the Julesburg route crosses half the mountains on this continent. It has to take Bridger Pass though the Rockies, and that's the highest pass in the chain. Right, Butler?"

Butler nodded slowly, and, although his bull-throated voice had been developed from cursing countless teams, it couldn't match Mackinaw's. "The California Trail goes through South Pass, and that's the lowest break in the Rockies, and it follows a river almost all the way. The Julesburg jumps from the South Platte and heads north across the Laramie Plains where there won't be any ready water for days on end . . . !"

He stopped yelling at them suddenly,

turning in a surprised way to Manton, who had just stepped into the open space. The gambler stood there a moment without speaking. Ringo made a half move forward from where he stood in front of Sol Lewis, mouth twisting into a drunken snarl. Arvada's face darkened. Then Manton spoke. His voice wasn't very loud, but the other sounds had quieted now, and it carried.

"Seems to me, working over any mountains would be a lot better than risking a wipe-out by Sioux. There's others here that know the trails just as well as Butler, if not better. How about it, Owhee?"

The buckskinned man was leaning on his long Jake Hawkins rifle in the front ranks; he spat, cackled. "Sure the gambler's right. I been traveling back and forth acrost the Oregon nigh onto twenty years now, and this is my last trip. I wanna get to Grande Ronde alive. I seen more than one train wiped out. Bodies layin' 'round with no hair, men spread-eagled on wagon wheels and sliced to ribbons with butcher knives, women . . ." — he broke off, looking at the few bonneted women in the crowd, then spat again — "well, anyways, it's a whole lot easier to climb a few mountains than to fight our way through every Oglala Sioux between here and the Green."

"Are you gonna listen to a tinhorn gambler and an old man in his second childhood?" interrupted Arvada. "Butler's traveled the region as much as Owhee. Those Indian rumors are always floating around. You'll be as safe on the California as you were back home in bed. There's twice as many forts along that northern route. . . ."

"Which should be plain proof that there's twice as many Indians," said Manton.

Owhee cackled again, and several more in the crowd laughed half-heartedly. Arvada took a step forward. For a moment, his black eyes flashed past the gambler to those half-dozen 'skinners who drove for him — then he was looking at Manton, and he bit off his words angrily.

"You keep out of this, Manton. Just because you knocked the red-eye out of Ringo the other day doesn't mean you can buck me forever. I've got four wagons in this train and that gives me a word in what goes on, but you don't own one damn' linchpin, and you haven't got a thing to say."

"That's right, tinhorn," said Sol Lewis. "You're horning in where you're not wanted."

There was a sullen mutter of assent from others. Manton could see how Arvada had split them already — men like Mackinaw and Owhee wanting to take the Julesburg, yet just as many others, like Sol Lewis, swayed by Arvada's smooth tongue.

"What's your stake in this, Arvada?" Manton asked suddenly. "Seems to me you should be anxious to take the safest route if you have wagons in the train. Or maybe you don't care about your wagons. Maybe you want the Sioux to lift our hair."

"Yeah," bellowed Mackinaw, "what is your stake in it?"

Some of the other emigrants began to shout, and Arvada looked swiftly around the circle. He tried to say something, but his voice was lost in the hubbub. Patently he was losing control over the crowd. He glanced toward his teamsters, behind Manton, and his eyes flashed with hot anger, and he jerked his head. The teamsters suddenly shoved forward against Manton, knocking him off balance, shouting.

"Take the gambler out of this."

"What's a tinhorn know about Injuns?"

"I vote for the California."

"The California, the California. . . ."

Stumbling forward before the weight of their shoving bodies, realizing what Arvada was doing, Manton lashed out backward with a boot. He felt it crunch into someone's knee, heard a sharp cry. Then he let himself go on forward, because, if it was going to be a fight, he wanted Arvada.

Apparently the Creole had the same idea. He had swung around and was shifting his legs wider apart to meet Manton.

Ringo was fighting through the crowd from the other side, too, getting his Patersons free. But the whole knot of men was whirling and shifting crazily, and half a dozen men were thrown in between Manton and Arvada, forcing Ringo back and ruining his chances for a shot. Cut off from Arvada like that, Manton crashed into the first man he could get his hands on. Clew Butler.

The wagon boss was thrown backward a couple of staggering paces by Manton's hurtling weight. Then he caught himself, and stopped like an oak rooted to the ground. Those teamsters came in from behind, and Manton was caught between them and Butler.

One of them grabbed Manton's arm, jerking it into a hammerlock; another piled on top of the gambler, sweaty hands grabbing at his face, twisting his head around, strangling, gagging. A third stuck a big boot between his churning legs, tripping him up. And Butler let a ham-like fist drive into Manton's belly.

Manton's breath exploded from him, and he bent over with pain, collapsed to a knee beneath the weight of the bodies. Then, down there where he was choked and half-blinded by the billowing dust, where all he could see was the blur of kicking, swinging boots, something caught hold of Manton. Leah thought he didn't have any emotion, thought he couldn't feel a hot rage boiling inside him, enveloping all his senses, a battle lust that spread over him like a wave and left no vestige of the old control, but she was wrong. Suddenly his black-coated figure was a raging, kicking, fighting thing that surged up from beneath Butler and Arvada's muleskinners — surged up with an explosive new strength given him by the sudden release of emotion that had been pent up so long. He heard his own crazy roar above Butler's bull bellow, above all the other tumult.

He twisted around and got one of the men on his back in a strangle hold, pulling him around and under with a yank, battering a fist into his face. At the same time he lunged forward into Butler, taking a blow on the mouth so he could get close enough to put a knee in the man's groin. Butler reeled back with a sick cry, and Manton released his strangle hold on the man he was hitting, digging a shoulder into his chest and heaving him off.

For an instant he had fought free, and he could see the rest of the milling, shifting crowd. No man could tell who was with Arvada, or who was with Manton. The whole bunch of them were slugging and kicking and knifing indiscriminately, women running around the fringe of the crowd, yelling shrilly and dragging at their husbands or brothers in a futile attempt to stop them.

Owhee's long Jake Hawkins appeared above the press an instant before it smashed down on a teamster's head, and the old scout's voice came to Manton, dry, cracked, wild: "Hang on, gambler, we're coming to he'p you. Hang on!"

As Manton turned to meet flailing fists, he heard a grizzly bellow from somewhere, and out of the fighting mess came Mackinaw Williams, the gigantic Arkansan. Nobody could stop his rush. Men staggered away from in front of him like water pluming from a ship's prow. A pair of hulking 'skinners converged on him. One he tossed high over the crowd, and the man screamed, and then the scream was stopped as he disappeared again into the shifting bodies. The other, Mackinaw kicked aside like a puppy. A bullwhacker came at the giant with a clubbed Ward-Burton. Mackinaw caught the rifle and snapped it like a match, then hit the man once in the face, and was past him before his body hit the ground.

A fist smashed Manton in the ribs. He lurched forward, grappling in close with a teamster, hooking him hard in the face. Fighting like that, he caught sight of Mackinaw again. In all that crowd, there had been only one man able to stop the giant. With skill learned long ago on the river, Georges Arvada had put himself in Mackinaw's path, had halted his juggernaut rush. They were locked together now, swaying back and forth, Mackinaw's thick arms around Arvada's square torso. Arvada was a big man, bigger than Manton. But the Arkansan towered over the Creole a full head, outweighed him fifty pounds.

Manton had seen Arvada fight years before on the river. He had been a skillful, terrible, deadly man to meet, and the *voyageur* lucky enough to live through a battle with him bore the scars of his boots the rest of his life. But no one else had been able to stop Mackinaw, and now Arvada was bent like a hickory bow in the Arkansan's bear hug, and his spine would snap in another instant.

Then the master of a hundred river battles

seemed to collapse. It took Mackinaw off guard, allowing Arvada to pull sideways in a swift, calculated movement. Mackinaw was forced to shift his grip. In that instant, Arvada snaked his right leg around behind Mackinaw, lunging up and forward. Levered backward by Arvada's full weight, Mackinaw had to take a step to the rear. He tripped over the Creole's leg.

Even before they hit the ground, Arvada was free of Mackinaw's weakened grip. He rolled away from the giant, bouncing to his feet, cat-like. Mackinaw tried to rise. But Arvada was already moving in with the skill and precision of a dancing master. Savate.

Mackinaw's knees were still bent when the Creole's heavy river boot lashed out head high and caught the giant on the tip of his chin. Mackinaw went over like a felled oak. Arvada's white teeth flashed in an evil, twisted grin, and he jumped for the fallen man.

Knowing what was coming, Manton pushed forward, rolling one of the 'skinners to the ground with a lucky roundhouse, lowering his head, and butting through another, trying desperately to reach Mackinaw and Arvada.

Yet, even as the 'skinner fell away from Manton's butting head, the gambler saw

Arvada come down on Mackinaw with both boots. The huge Arkansan tried to roll free. Arvada rode him as he would birl a log in whitewater, dancing from the back of his neck to the side of his head as he rolled, then tromping full in his face as he came belly up.

Mackinaw bellowed with pain, jerked spasmodically, hands coming up and pawing for Arvada's boots. The Creole avoided those hands and came down again on the giant's bloody face. Mackinaw jerked once more, then lay still.

Butler reeled up in front of Manton then, blocking him from Arvada, and those teamsters hit from behind again. He felt the wagon boss' fist hit him in the face. Blood filled his mouth. Then a gun hit him on the back of the head, and sight and sound and smell blended into the blackness of pain, and the last thing he saw was Georges Arvada's evil, white-toothed smile, triumphant.

Five 🐂

Ed Manton woke to sounds that had become part of the pattern forming his existence — the endless, muted play of wheels beneath hub caps; the half-heard cursing of weary bullwhackers; the flap of some Osnaburg sheeting a driver had neglected to lash down. And the dust, the eternal dust, creeping through either end of the tilt, sifting into the semi-gloom with vagrant rays of sun picking out a few swirling motes.

His head throbbed, and, when he reached up, there was the soft feel of cotton bandages. He sat up and thought he would faint for a moment. The spell passed, and, looking forward, he could see Leah's yellow curls shining below her sunbonnet. He crawled painfully over the big armchair Nestor had brought for his house, across the box of china and the roll of calico Leah had insisted on taking along for curtains.

She turned as he poked his head out from under the front hoop. "Thank goodness you've come around. You were unconscious all last night and this morning. I was worried. And you get back in there and lie down."

He hiked his scarred boots over the back of the box seat. "I'm all right. How did I get out of that alive?"

"Beatrie saved you," she said. "Fought his way through and held them off with his gun. They would have trampled you to death, I guess, or shot you while you lay there. He couldn't stop the fight, but he pulled you free. With you and Mackinaw out of it, Arvada had everything about his own way."

He rubbed his head ruefully. "I guess I didn't do so well."

"You were marvelous," she said hotly. "It doesn't matter so much whether you won or lost. You got mad. That's what matters. I could hear you yelling clear outside. You just about killed one of Arvada's teamsters, and you messed up a couple of others so they won't be able to skin any mules for a long time."

He was looking at his hands, and he spoke without lifting his eyes. "Leah, do you think a man who was set in his ways . . . a man who'd lived one sort of a life so long he'd forgotten any other . . . do you think he could change?"

She hauled on the reins suddenly. Traces quivered, then sagged as the mules halted.

The wagons ahead had stopped, and Manton could see teamsters hitching reins around whipstocks all down the line, and jumping from their wagons. They gathered into a little knot and moved back toward Leah's wagon. They were mostly the men who had followed Nestor, big, slow-moving farmers, faces grimy and wind-burned.

Leah motioned toward them. "There's your answer. I told you they never understood you because you hid behind that mask all the time. You came out from behind it last night, and they saw you. And now, if you want it, here's the chance to change from those ways you were set in."

Mackinaw seemed to have been chosen spokesman; his face was covered with white bandaging, and his words were muffled. "Manton, ever since Nestor died, we've needed someone to lead us. Arvada tried to shove Clew Butler in last night. The Creole had already convinced some of us with his smooth tongue, and, after the fight, there was some more sided with him because he'd won. But there's still a few of us left who were Nestor's friends. We don't trust Arvada or Butler. I guess we didn't trust you, either. But Nestor did, and we can see why now."

"But I didn't do any good last night. . . ."

"Hell," spat a thick-necked bullwhacker, breaking in on Manton, "every good man loses once in a while. You were the only one with guts enough to stand out there and face Arvada and his crew. That's enough for me."

"We've come to the fork in the trail," said Mackinaw, "and we still want to take the Julesburg route. Without you, we won't be worth much against the Creole. . . ."

The drum of hoofs turned them. Arvada reined up his big jughead in a cloud of his own dust. Ringo was with him, bright sun catching the silver mounting on his saddle.

"What's up, gentlemen?" asked Arvada, grinning balefully at Manton.

The emigrants shifted nervously, glancing at the gambler, silent. Suddenly Manton stood up on the footboards of the high box seat. He felt weak, shaky, but his voice was strong.

"We're taking the Julesburg route, Arvada."

"I thought all that was settled last night," said the Creole.

"Nothing was settled," said Manton.

"The majority decided the California was the fork to take," Arvada said. "You have to abide by their decision."

"If it had been decided right," said

Manton, "maybe we would abide by it. But it wasn't put to any vote. You bulled it through with your strong-arm boys. Whoever wants to take the California with you can take it. We're for Julesburg."

Arvada suddenly wheeled his mare and spurred her into the crowd, scattering the men. "Get back to your wagons. The fork is just ahead, and anybody that doesn't take the California will be inviting a chunk of lead through his brisket."

"Arvada!" Manton's voice was commanding. He had slipped Nestor's Springfield from beneath the box seat and was holding it across his belly. He was a big man, standing there with the tails of his coat whipped about his long legs by the wind, the sunlight falling hard across the craggy planes of his face. They were all watching him now. "Let's not start another ruckus . . . it might not come out like the one last night," he said. Then he turned to the men. "You go back to your wagons all right. I guess you know which fork to take when we come to it."

Ringo set quiescent, bleary eyes on the Springfield, hands carefully high from his guns. Arvada watched the men filter back toward their wagons for a long moment. He held his reins in one big, dark hand, and

Manton saw it begin to tremble. The Creole suddenly slapped that hand onto his pommel, knuckles growing white with the force of his grip, and he turned a gradually darkening face up to the gambler. He opened his mouth as if to speak, then closed it again, taking a deep breath.

"I guess there've been enough mistakes in your life, Manton," he said finally, his voice shaking through white lips. "You'll find out soon enough this was the biggest one you ever made."

Then he wheeled his horse and rode toward the front of the line, disappearing at last in the billowing clouds of white alkali dust.

It was mountain country beyond Julesburg, new country to Manton. They had split at the fork, the gambler leading eight creaking wagons southward, Arvada and Sol Lewis and the rest of the train taking the California Trail. And now, Manton and Owhee and Beatrie rode together ahead of the wagons almost every day. They rode through groves of mountain mahogany where brown juncos whirred up in startled flight from the rabbit brush. They rode past salt flats where white-rumped pronghorns stood watching them till they were very close, then bounced away into the cool timber.

The oxen and mules were showing the strain of the long haul. Men were kept busy greasing gall sores with tallow and gunpowder, putting new shoes on, watching for lumpy jaw and the other diseases that caught at an exhausted animal with its lowered resistance. The high, dry air shrunk wagon boxes and wheels, and evening camps were filled with the tattoo of teamsters knocking iron tires back onto warped rims. The men, too, were taking on a gaunt look. It showed most in Manton, because he was the leader now, and it was all on his shoulders. He had lost weight; his belly was as hard and flat as when he'd been a kid, swamping on the docks at St. Louis. His face was as dark as an Indian's, fair hair bleached almost as white as Beatrie's by the sun.

Granite Cañon with its spring of ice water passed behind their rumbling wheels, and Laramie Plains with its endless expanse of rabbit brush and greasewood flats — and then Bridger Pass, not as high or as hard as Butler had claimed, yet difficult enough to make the teamsters throw themselves, exhausted, into sougans the night they gained the western slope. After that came the dry, hot, maddening stretch of alkali around Barrel Springs, where the animals had to have their mouths and nostrils swabbed with precious water every half hour to keep them from choking to death. And finally, Fort Bridger on Black's Fork of the Green.

Old Jim Bridger had built his log houses and stockade in the shelter of tall, olive-yellow poplars that filled the air with a sweet, resinous scent, and Manton rode gratefully into their shade. The wagons parked in the grove, and 'skinners un-hitched jaded teams to water them in the river. Manton unsaddled the sorrel, pick-eted it near Leah's Conestoga. He and Owhee were the first to head toward the wall of boulderstone with its sharp pickets on top that marked the fort.

A few Crow Indians squatted around the big, brass-bound gate, smoking red and yellow longpipes. Their tobacco was made from the inner bark of the willow and called *kinnikinnick;* the smell of it gagged Manton. Dogs began yapping from inside the walls, and a bearded Yankee pushed open the wicket in the big gate. Two or three mon-grels burst out around him and came to sniff the gambler, and growl. Then another man followed the first out. A long, bald scare-crow of a man in tattered homespun held up by galluses, a blood-stained bandage around his head, left arm in a soiled sling.

Manton took an uncertain step forward, then broke into a run, calling: "Lewis! Sol Lewis!"

Leah and Beatrie were right behind him, and the others. They crowded around the lanky man, shouting questions. He waited patiently till they quieted down, eyes dull, cast down.

"We met Indians on the California all right," he said finally. "They wiped the train out."

There was a long, stunned silence, then Manton asked: "Arvada?"

Lewis shook his head. "Just before we hit the Indians, Arvada's lead wagon dished a wheel. His four outfits were the last in line, and he said for us to go on and he'd catch up at the evening camp. Five or six miles farther on, Sioux hit us. We didn't even have time to corral. My horse was shot and fell on me, knocked me out. I guess the only thing that saved me was my bald head. When I came to, it was all over."

"Funny Arvada should stay behind with all his wagons for the one that dished a wheel. Did the Indians get him?" asked Manton.

"I don't know," said Lewis. "We were

going to stop the whole train till he got that wheel fixed, seein' as we were in the Indian country. But he insisted on us going ahead. The Indians ran off all our stock, but there was still a couple of mules running around when I got out from under my horse. I grabbed one and headed over South Pass and down the Green. And Arvada hasn't passed here yet."

"Ten to one the Sioux got him, too," said Beatrie. "I don't see how they could miss."

"On any other bet," said Manton, "I'd take those odds."

There was no doctor at Bridger, and Sol Lewis wasn't doing so well by the time the train had crossed the Bear River Divide. The surprise attack and the long, grueling ride from the scene of the massacre had told on him; his arm was swollen and infected, and he was rapidly getting weaker. The trail passed Bear Springs about half a mile away, and Manton decided to take Lewis into town to see what could be done. It was one of the oldest settlements on the trail, at the northern bend of the Bear River, surrounded by russet-colored hills, covered by green fir and mottled cedar. Beatrie and Owhee were already scouting ahead when Manton left the train, so only he and Lewis rode into the Springs. They hadn't had milled flour since Dobytown, and Leah asked Manton to get some while he was in town. The doctor had his office above the pharmacy at the north end of the main street. Manton left Lewis there and went south toward the sutler's store just outside Fort Conner at the other end of the street.

Summer heat hung over the buildings like a thick, stifling blanket, and the walks were empty of life except for an infrequent old man dozing in the sun, or someone hurrying from one patch of shade to another. Somehow, the large group of dusty riders in front of the frame store didn't fit with the rest of the lazy scene.

They all packed saddle guns in fringed scabbards, and short guns that sagged heavy against worn, leather leggings or brush-scarred trousers. Two or three stood around nervously smoking cigarettes, wiping sweat-caked faces; the others remained in their saddles, the weariness of a hard ride in their sagging bodies. With a glance at their narrow-eyed, hard-bitten faces, Manton moved into the store. It was a long moment before his eyes accustomed themselves to the gloom. Then he saw that the store itself comprised but half the big room. The other part was a taproom. A stairway led to a second story balcony, and from the part of the taproom that was hidden by those stairs came the muted buzz of talk, the clinking of glasses. Manton moved toward the plank counter with its row of cracker barrels.

"Got any milled flour?" he asked.

The clerk adjusted his spectacles. "Sure. If you're coming through with the wagons, I reckon you'll want a hundred-pound sack. That'll last you to Fort Boise. . . ."

But Manton had ceased to listen. Another voice had entered his consciousness. He couldn't place it at first.

"Twin Falls is the place, Knox. Nobody ever gets down to the bottom. Nobody's ever seen the bottom. The spray hides it. Must be a thousand-foot drop. The trail goes right along the edge. Drive the wagons over, teams and all. . . ."

Manton turned slowly. Georges Arvada was coming around from behind the stairs, still talking, followed by a small group: Johnny Ringo, Clew Butler, and a tall, cadaverous gent in a purple fustian. As he rounded the banister, Arvada looked up. For a moment he trailed off. Then a slow, baleful grin spread across his dark face.

"I thought maybe you'd got by those Indians at South Pass," said Manton. "Dish any more wheels on the way in, Arvada?"

"No. No, I didn't," said Arvada. "We were just going to sit in on a little draw, Manton. Care to join us?"

Manton shook his head. "I never play cards."

Arvada laughed. It wasn't pleasant. "I don't think it would be polite of you to refuse my invitation. No, I don't think it would be polite at all."

There were two others behind Ringo. One was a dusty hardcase, so like those others outside, and the other a big, portly man with long side-whiskers and a Prince Albert coat. Manton sensed death closing in around him now. Ringo was swaying back and forth, swacked to the gills. Manton had a good idea what would happen if he refused to play their card game. There would be no percentage in forcing anything now, not with all five of them waiting for him to do just that. He looked at the man in the purple fustian. Arvada caught the glance.

"The gentleman in the purple coat is Mister Knox of the Diamond Hall and the Naked Truth," said the Creole, "in case you're interested."

"I am," said Manton. "I figure it's about time somebody introduced him to me."

Arvada motioned toward the taproom. "Shall we?"

Manton didn't let anybody get behind him as the Creole led around the stairs to where they had been sitting before, out of sight of the store. Ringo took a chair opposite Manton. Arvada sat to his right, Knox to his left. Manton started to sit down. The portly gentleman and the dusty rider were still standing, and they began to sidle around behind the gambler. Manton's chair made a loud, scraping noise as he shoved it back, rising again. He moved his claw hammer away from the black butt of his gun with an elbow.

"Let's not have any watchers," he said.

Maybe Arvada didn't want to start the thing then, or maybe he wasn't sure just how good Manton had become with that Navy revolver. He looked at its black handle, then grinned.

"The gambler's right, boys," he said mockingly. "Don't stand behind him . . . you don't have to."

No, thought Manton bitterly, *you don't have to . . . there are enough of you in front of me.* When the men moved to one side, behind Knox, Manton sat down again. There was nothing else to do really.

Ringo slipped a deck of cards from the pocket of his leather vest and dealt each man a hand. Five cards, face down. Draw.

Arvada took his hand and spread it, grinning at Manton. Knox spread his cards without looking at them. Ringo, too, was watching Manton, fanning his hand automatically.

"You gave me only one card," said Manton.

Ringo nodded. "That's right. Draw it."

Manton palmed the card and turned it up. It was the ace of spades.

♪ Six

In the utter silence that followed, Manton raised his eyes slowly to meet Ringo's. "Bart Nestor's notch is on *your* gun, then."

Arvada answered for his man. "That's what I like about you, Manton. You have such a quick mind . . . you catch on so fast."

"I sort of had Mister Knox here pegged as the gent who cashed in Nestor's chips," said Manton. "The bartender at the Naked Truth had a vague recollection of a man in a purple fustian."

"Oh, Knox was there," said Arvada, then he nodded toward the portly man in the dark Prince Albert. "I had the colonel, here, invite Nestor to a little stud. When the game was going good, Knox drifted in. If Nestor remembered him from Diamond Hall, there wasn't much he could do, then, was there? And because Knox muffed it at the Hall, I had Ringo accidentally wander by. Just to make sure, you see. Ringo was a good boy. He sat in on a hand, and he didn't muff anything."

"Why go to all that trouble?" asked

Manton. "Why not just shoot Nestor down in the street?"

Arvada's eyebrows went up in a mocking way. "But, Manton, that would be . . . murder. If I'm going to build a town in Grande Ronde, I can't have such an ugly word soiling my coat tails till I'm in good and solid. The same way here. Just a little card game behind the stairs where the clerk can't see. Somebody gets mad about something, and, when the smoke clears away. . . ."

He didn't have to finish. Manton could remember how Nestor had looked there at Dobytown, young head resting on the table, three holes in his back, fingers spread out over the ace of spades in the dead man's hand.

"I take it you constituted the syndicate that tried to buy out Nestor in Omaha," said Manton through thinned lips.

"You take it right . . . the colonel was my front man, and Nestor never knew I was in it," said Arvada. "A marvelous spot, Grande Ronde. It'll drag ten times the chips Omaha did. And I won't have to take any third. No Big Three running things. Just a Big One. Me. Bart Nestor and his friends happened to get there ahead of me and sew the valley up with their fool homesteads. But then, when you're out for the big pot, you always have to go to some trouble, don't you, Manton? I got rid of Nestor so I could turn that wagon train onto the California. The Sioux had wiped out two parties before Nestor's. It was almost a certain thing. And nobody could blame me for what a bunch of Indians did to those homesteaders, could they?"

"Only you didn't quite finish the job," said Manton.

Ringo began laying his cards down, one by one, the first slapping against the table flatly. A tight, pale look came into the colonel's face. Knox's lips curled into that sardonic smile. Manton suddenly realized what would happen when Ringo's last card lit the table.

"No," said Arvada. "No, I didn't quite finish the job, thanks to you. And I won't be able to let the Indians keep my coat tails clean now, will I? But, then, I have the colonel's help. He's a Bear Springs man himself, and those boys outside are his. And my 'skinners are camped just outside the fort. That gives me enough to handle the job, I think."

Ringo slapped his second card down. Knox took his right hand from his pasteboards, and Manton remembered the gun beneath that fustian.

Arvada laughed, then went on. "I was just telling Knox here what an ideal spot Twin Falls is. Your wagons pass by there this afternoon. It's in the gorge of the Snake, a few miles west of where Bear River flows into it. The spray from the falls hides the bottom of the gorge, and nobody's ever seen it."

Ringo slapped his third card down. Up to now, Manton hadn't considered escape. There were too many of them here. He had thought of it simply as trying to match Ringo's draw when it came, and of getting one or two slugs into somebody before they put his lights out. Now he could see it wasn't that simple. If he didn't get away to warn the train, Arvada would still have his boom town in Grande Ronde.

The Creole was talking on: "The trail runs right near the edge, for quite a ways, cliffs on one side, gorge on the other. If the mules were stampeded, they couldn't run any place but right over into that gorge. And mules do stampede so easy, don't they, Manton?" He laughed nastily.

Manton had the picture of three spans of kicking mules being stampeded off into the pale green haze of the gorge by those dusty, yellow hardcases of the colonel's, and of the huge Conestoga smashing over behind them, and of a woman's yellow hair caught in the wind an instant before the whole outfit disappeared into that rising spray forever.

Ringo put his fourth card down.

Arvada's grin was tight and fixed on his face now. Knox's right hand was a tense, waiting claw. Sweat broke through the dust caked on the face of the hard-bitten man standing beside the colonel.

Ringo's hand was lifting to slap down his last card.

Manton had seen a huge drunken rail-splitter do it once in St. Louis. There had been a half a dozen men at the table, and it had taken every one of them. It was a good trick, if a man had the strength and timed it right. The gambler could feel the muscles tightening throughout his body, and his face set into that expressionless mask.

Ringo slapped the fifth card onto the table.

They all moved at once. Knox's right hand flashed for his coat. The colonel took a lurching step backward to get out of the way. Arvada bent forward to rise. Ringo went for his Patersons where he sat. And Manton did what he'd seen that rail-splitter do. His knees unbent like hinges snapping open. A grunt exploded from him with the terrific effort he put forth. He came up with the heavy table, heaving it over on all of them.

Arvada wheezed and doubled over as the edge caught him in the middle. Ringo went down underneath, fancy-topped Justins kicking. Knox tried to shove his chair back and get out of the way at the same time. He tripped on the chair, sprawled into the colonel, and they both went down in a tangle.

The colonel's man was the only one to escape. He jumped backward, but the edge was taken off his draw by surprise. Manton's hand flashed to his Navy. It came out much faster than he had expected. His thumb had the hammer eared back before the muzzle cleared leather, and the hair trigger jumped beneath his finger, and the man took the slug square in his middle.

Manton was halfway to the end of the stairs by the time Knox fought free of the colonel and came to his knees, hand dipping beneath his coat once more. The other time it had been a Derringer. This time it was a Navy .36 with an eight-inch barrel and a big, black handle that bucked again against Manton's palm as he got his second shot out. The man in the purple fustian fell sideways across the chair he had already knocked over, crashing to the floor.

Then Manton was outside, yelling some garbled gibberish at those riders waiting there, pointing back in through the door. They reacted without thinking, three or four of them breaking for the store. They were almost inside when they stopped, crowding up against each other, turning back with puzzled faces. One of them yelled at Manton.

"What?"

Another yelled: "Who . . . ?"

But the big man was already half a block down the street, claw hammer flapping out behind him. Sol Lewis was standing in front of the pharmacy, by the two horses. When he saw Manton coming in a run like that, and Arvada plunging out of the sutler's store, he scrambled onto his own mount and came toward Manton at a gallop, leading the sorrel. Manton caught the reins flung at him, jumped into the saddle, wheeled the sorrel.

"It's Arvada . . . Ringo!" he shouted. "Get back to the wagons!"

They clattered out of the town, turning into a cut through the foothills that led to the trail. Arvada and his men showed at the north of Bear Springs' main street just as Lewis and Manton disappeared into the first stunted firs on the gentle slope.

The men the colonel had brought bore signs of a long ride, and their horses would be jaded already. The long haul from the Missouri had gaunted Manton's sorrel, but had molded it, too. And now it showed its steel beneath Manton's raking spurs, taking the bit in its teeth and stretching out. They topped a saddle and thundered down the north slope onto the wheel-rutted Oregon Trail, then turned northwest toward the confluence of the Bear and the Snake.

Behind them, on the ridge, showed the silhouettes of Arvada's riders, urging weary beasts into a wind-blown run.

✦ Seven

The gorge of the Snake River had been sculptured from the beginning of time by volcanic upheavals and erosion and glaciers. Riding the trail along its lip toward Twin Falls was to Manton like galloping through a nightmare. Huge, black monoliths of lava flashed past his horse, and russet-colored turrets of sandstone, and bizarre mosques tinted crimson by the afternoon sun. At times, he could see into the gorge itself, a thick haze of spray lying over its bottom and hiding the river.

They galloped through a desolate formation of rocks, hoofs sounding hollow, striking sparks, then past a series of small blue lakes that stretched southward beyond sight. And all the time, Manton was seeing that Conestoga tumbling into the gorge after a kicking, squealing team of mules, and a woman's yellow hair, caught by the wind.

Finally he became conscious of a sullen roaring over the pound of his mount's hoofs. It took him a moment to recognize what it was. Then he knew Twin Falls was ahead.

They galloped around a towering abutment of sandstone and caught sight of the wagons. Manton's shout was lost in the growing roar of water. Beneath him, in the gorge, he could see the huge, basaltic horse-shoe with the water pouring over it like a great flood of white snow, smashing against the gleaming south wall of the cañon and rolling away in pale green veins that fell into the enveloping haze of foam below. Owhee was the first to see Manton, then Beatrie, and they wheeled their mounts back.

"Arvada!" Manton shouted at them. "Stop the wagons. Arvada's coming with his bunch to stampede you over into the gorge."

Neither of the men heard him because of the roar of the falls, and he had to repeat it in a scream as they sidled their horses into his. Then they whirled and raced back to the wagons, Manton following on his weary, jaded sorrel. By the time he reached Leah's Conestoga, the men and women had gathered there, waiting for him. He swung off his horse onto the box seat. For a moment, he and Leah were looking at each other, and he could see her lips moving, saying one word. "Ed."

Then he turned and shouted down at the emigrants. "Arvada's coming to wipe us out. Anybody doesn't want to come with me can back out. I'm picking the men I want and am going to meet him. The rest of you corral the wagons."

He took all the men he dared, leaving a bare handful to defend the wagons in case Arvada got through them. Beatrie, of course, with his deadly skill. Owhee, who could count coup for every half ounce of Galena lead that left his long Jake Hawkins. Mackinaw, who still bore Arvada's caulk marks on his face. Sol Lewis could only use one arm, but he pleaded so that Manton finally gave in and let him go, too. And finally a pair of hulking, red-shirted 'skinners who were better than average with short guns. Seven men against Arvada's small army, but Manton knew every one of them to the core, and he had bluffed out aces with three spots before.

Someone shouted, and pointed to the crazy jumble of rocks that formed the rim of the cliffs beside the trail. Manton saw a man sitting a piebald pony up there, a man in a silver-mounted saddle, swaying slightly as if blown by the breeze.

"All right," yelled the gambler, "let's go!"

The whole chain of jagged foothills was the result of a volcanic upheaval that had happened millennia ago, and the jumble of lava uplifts and piles of granite and sandstone that covered the slope made it possible for both forces to move within a few yards of each other without being seen.

The cliffs formed a sheer drop of thirty feet, and the only way up to the jagged slopes above was via two parallel cañons that cut down through the cliff and opened out onto the trail. The pair of cañons formed three ridges, and dictated an obvious strategy. Whoever took the center ridge commanded both cañons and thus had control over the entrance from the trail into the cliffs, or the exit from the cliffs onto the trail. Arvada wouldn't be blind to that. Crouching in the shadows of a huge boulder, hidden from above, Manton put his mouth close to Owhee's ear and pointed to a crazy mass of rocks a hundred yards up the center ridge.

"Do you think you could hold Arvada there till I work around above and come down the ridge from behind him?"

Owhee spat, grinned. "Sol Lewis is a good shot with that Springfield of his. Gimme him, and I'll lay so much Galena lead across that ridge Arvada'll wish he never heard of Grande Ronde."

Manton told Lewis, then watched the two of them squirm through a sandy gully and into the mouth of the cañon, working up its side to the ridge. Then he took Mackinaw and Beatrie and the two muleskinners and moved up the other side of the cañon to the far ridge. The earth trembled beneath him from the force of the thousands of tons of water plunging over the falls into the gorge below, and the roar of that same water drowned all other sound, and the sun cast long shadows behind the weird formations of gleaming, red rocks. He crawled through a strata of forbidding black lava, as smooth and slick as greasy buckskin, then over sandstone that crumbled beneath his hands. He gained the ridge, and could look across the cañon and see Owhee and Lewis working into their position. Then he led his men into the jumbled rocks and twisted mat of stunted cedar, taking cover that prevented him from seeing that center ridge, and that prevented Arvada from seeing him.

They worked up toward the peaks of the rugged hills until Manton guessed they were past Arvada. Then they cut down into the cañon, which had narrowed till it was almost a fissure, and up the other steep side. They moved slowly and carefully as they neared the center ridge, flitting like shadows from rock to rock, cleft to cleft. And one by one they crawled on their bellies over the rimrock and onto the top. Lying there, Manton caught a red shirt down below, and he knew he was above Arvada.

Manton was breathing hard from the climb, but his heart began to beat faster with something more than the physical effort as he started to move on down toward the Creole. He couldn't hear his own men behind him because of the roaring of the falls, but he knew also that Arvada wouldn't be able to hear him. Then he crawled around a lava uplift, and Arvada's men were spread out before him across the narrow ridge.

The Creole, with four of his red-shirted muleskinners, lay behind a long sawtooth of granite. One of those 'skinners was on his back, sightless eyes staring up, and that would be due to Owhee's long Jake Hawkins. The colonel sprawled on his portly belly behind a boulder, a pair of his dusty riders with him, all carrying their saddle guns.

Even as Manton was coming from behind that rock, he saw another of those hard-bitten men scuttle from a fissure, in a doubled-over run heading for where the colonel lay. He didn't make any discernible noise when it happened. He just threw up his arms and went over on his face, sliding down the ridge on his belly until he came up against a rock that stopped him — and that would be Owhee's long Jake Hawkins, too.

Then Manton realized Johnny Ringo was nowhere to be seen. Some animal sense of danger clawing at him, he turned back up the ridge. Filtering out from the garish red rocks above Manton was the drunken trigger artist, swaying precariously from side to side, and his mouth was open in a yell that had no sound.

Behind him was Clew Butler, pulling a big Ward-Burton against his belly for a spot shot. And back of him were three of the colonel's Bear Springs men.

Screaming at his bunch to turn around, Manton tried to whirl farther so his shot would be square. But that hair-trigger was for a slap-leather draw, and the gun jumped beneath his hand before he had lined it up, and he missed Johnny Ringo completely. Then it was all the crazy madness of silent battle. Manton saw one of his own teamsters go down before Butler's flaming Ward-Burton. Then Butler was clubbing his single-shot rifle and thundering past the man he had nailed, gun slamming back over his shoulder for a vicious swing at Manton.

The gambler threw himself forward, trying to duck in under the blow and get a blind shot at Butler's belly. The rifle caught him square on the back, sending pain in a flood through his whole body. But he smashed on up against Butler, carrying him back against Mackinaw, who had grappled with that trio of the colonel's men. They all slammed to the ground in a kicking, swearing tangle. Manton's rush carried them backward as they fell, and the whole struggling mess of men slid off that narrow ridge.

The slope was steep, and there was nothing to do but roll clear down to the bottom, smashing through rabbit brush and bouncing off jagged rocks. Manton felt the weight of a man hit him once, then was freed again as the body rolled over his own hurtling form. Finally he slammed into the sandy bottom and lay there, stunned, groaning.

It took a terrible effort to rise. By some nameless instinct he had hung onto his gun. He shook his head dazedly, swaying on hands and knees, looking up. Twenty feet above him, on the same sandy floor of the cañon, was Mackinaw Williams. He was already on his feet, the center of a struggling bunch of the men he had taken off the ridge with him. One of the dusty hardcases lay sprawled beneath the pounding, kicking boots, apparently killed by the fall. But the other two, and Clew Butler, were writhing madly with the giant Arkansan.

Manton saw a saddle gun go up and down like a piston, saw Mackinaw's head jerk beneath the blow. Then one of the colonel's men was slammed back against the cañon wall, body hitting with a silent impact.

Another man whirled out of the fight, holding his head and screaming soundlessly. Mackinaw caught Clew Butler around the body in that bear hug. The big wagon boss stiffened, head jerking back, face twisted with pain. The man who had just reeled away from Mackinaw began to grab for his short gun.

Swaying erect, Manton broke into a slogging run, trying to line his Navy up. But the man got his six-shooter free and spread his legs, holding it with both hands. It bucked and bucked and bucked. Manton saw the giant jerk with each shot, and refuse to go down. When the man's gun was empty, he lurched in behind Williams and slugged desperately at his head.

Manton was close now. Mackinaw took the first blow and shuddered from head to foot, still gripping Butler in those terrible arms. He took the second one and sagged, face sinking onto Butler's chest. The man raised his gun for a third time. Then Manton was near enough to hit what he shot at, and his .36 recoiled in his hand. The man stopped, his gun in mid-air above Mackinaw's head, and fell backward.

Mackinaw went to his knees, dropping Butler against the side of the cañon. The wagon boss collapsed like a rag doll, dead eyes looking blankly at the giant who rocked back and forth on his knees above. Before Manton could reach him, Mackinaw fell on top of the man he had crushed to death.

The gambler swayed there for a long moment with his smoking gun in his hand before he realized he was the only one alive in that narrow, steep-walled cañon. Mackinaw was dead, and he had killed Butler and two of the others. The man Manton had shot was dead.

Manton put his gun away and began the slow, painful climb back up to the ridge. The rocks had torn his coat to ribbons, had ripped chunks from his flesh. Each move was fresh pain. Finally he reached the top.

Only the dead and wounded lay on the ridge. Arvada and the colonel and the others had disappeared. Manton moved down, passing the sawtooth of granite where the Creole had lain. The roaring of the falls began to enter his consciousness again, and he felt the ground trembling beneath his feet once more. He came to a bare, open space where the ridge broadened and, rather than expose himself, worked down into the cañon again, climbing along the steep wall. He found a lateral fissure and used it for cover. A few feet farther on it was choked with scrub oak; he broke through the stunted trees onto a small, granite bench that overlooked a dizzy drop. On the harsh rock of that bench, belly down, lay Vern Beatrie.

His hand still held his gun, and the gun was still in its holster. Manton knelt, rolled him over, bent closely over him. The blond man opened his eyes, laughed weakly.

"That damn' Ringo got me. Lost him in the fight up there on the ridge. Butler got one of your 'skinners. The other one and me got a couple of those men with Arvada and scattered the rest. Then I spotted Ringo and Arvada and the colonel working down here into the cañon, followed 'em down that crack, broke through the scrub oak like you did. Ringo was there, surprised as I was. Even steven on the draw . . . both of us had our irons leathered." He laughed bitterly, choked, coughed up blood. "He took me before I even got my gun free. It's your job now, Manton. You can do it. You're a natural. Only take off that damn' claw hammer. . . ."

The voice failed.

"Beatrie!"

Manton didn't say any more. What could he say? Beatrie was dead.

Manton rose, a harsh, bleak look on his sweat-caked face. Riding with a man across half a continent that way, making camp with him or laughing at him when his horse puffed up under the cinch or getting mad at him when he wouldn't get up and light the fire in the morning, you couldn't help forming an attachment. Maybe Beatrie had been a killer. That didn't matter much now. Manton only knew the blond man had been his friend, as Nestor had been his friend. Now he was dead, as Nestor was dead. And Ringo had killed them.

Manton slipped off his claw hammer and laid it across Beatrie's face. Then he turned and moved across the bench after his man. He had no illusions as to what he was facing. Beatrie had been one of the best short-gun artists on the frontier, yet Ringo had edged him out on an even go. But Ringo had showed his yellow streak once before when Manton had knocked the red-eye out of him. And Manton wondered now, if all this climbing wouldn't sweat a lot of liquor from a man. Or, if not a lot, enough, at least, to take the edge off . . . ?

There were two boulders ahead, and Manton had to use both hands to keep from sliding off the smooth, round surface. He put his gun away and crawled in between them, one jutting above, one below. He slid out from beneath the top one, and Johnny Ringo stood on a narrow ledge that ran six feet beyond the rocks.

His hands were raised, grabbing an outgrowth of dusty juniper to pull himself up, and he was half faced toward Manton. When he saw the gambler, his hands lowered, and he began to sway.

Manton slid carefully over the bulge of rock, feet hitting the steep slope. Then, braced against the boulder that way, he set himself. Ten feet between them, and the ground trembling underfoot, and the roar of the falls enveloping all other sound.

"This is for Nestor, Ringo, this is for Beatrie, so go ahead and draw, damn you, go ahead and draw!"

But Ringo continued to sway, like a pendulum gaining momentum, hands a pale threat above his guns. Manton felt sweat break through the caked blood on his palm. The hardest part was the waiting.

"Draw, damn you!"

Ringo drew. Swaying forward, his hands dipped. Manton's mind went blank then. He wasn't consciously aware of diving, or crouching, or slapping for his Navy. He didn't even feel the gun in his hand till it exploded under that hair trigger.

He stood there a moment, feeling suddenly the smooth, black butt in his bloody hand, index finger still holding the trigger back tight from the first shot, thumb hovering over the hammer. And he looked at Johnny Ringo in dull disbelief.

The man still swayed on that narrow ledge. His guns were in his hands, but they were pointed down. As Manton watched, one silver-inlaid Paterson slid from those pale fingers, then the other, hitting against the steep side of the cañon without a sound and bouncing on down. Ringo followed them. He collapsed suddenly and went off the ledge into space, fancy-topped Justins kicking upward.

∩ Eight

Shale suddenly slapped into Manton's face, stinging. Spitting grit from between his teeth, he jerked his head up. Georges Arvada and the colonel had just worked around a lava bulge in the cañon wall to where they could see Manton, and the Creole was throwing down for another shot. Manton lurched forward along that ledge, ducking beneath the scrub oak as Arvada's second slug kicked up shale where he had stood a moment before.

The colonel and Arvada had patently been trying to outflank Owhee. Manton snapped a shot through the oak, saw his bullet puff sandstone a foot away from Arvada's thick belly. The Creole must have realized what an exposed position he was in. Sending a third wild shot at Manton, he clawed back around that lava bulge. The colonel wasn't so quick. He made a big target, on down the cañon wall and slightly above Manton, trying to follow Arvada around that bulge. Manton held his Navy at arm's length and got that dark Prince Albert square across his sights. Then he touched the trigger.

Above the thunder of the falls, the explosion was dull and muffled even to Manton. He saw the colonel jerk to the slug, then begin to slide down. His heavy body caught on a tough outgrowth of cedar and hung there, head dangling on one side, feet on the other.

It was a crazy fight after that. Manton moved out of the scrub oak, working upward behind a strata of granite. Arvada snapped a shot at him. Manton returned it and saw the Creole jerk back into cover. Manton reloaded, and they worked on down the cañon that way, exchanging shots, dodging, clawing, climbing. The steep wall became a slope, then a more gentle uplift, covered with matted growths of cedar. Arvada took to the stunted trees to gain on Manton. Following him through at a run, Manton broke into the open on a level. Quite far ahead, half hidden by a greenish haze that rose from the gorge, he saw the figure of Arvada. Running after him, Manton stumbled in a ditch. Then he realized it wasn't a ditch at all, but a wheel rut. He was on the trail again, around a turn from the wagons, where that second cañon came out through the cliffs. And across the trail was the gorge of the Snake River . . . and Arvada.

There were more rocks on the edge of the gorge, a whole stretch of them, as if some giant hand had thrown them carelessly there. Arvada's gun flamed from among them. With lead popping into turf a foot from him, Manton threw himself for the safety of the first big boulder. It would be the same thing all over now, the dodging, the futile shots. One thing was different, though. Arvada would have to stop at the gorge.

The greenish haze of foam hung above the red rocks like a thick fog, and the roaring waters seemed to be inside Manton's head now. He moved forward, unable to hear his own footsteps, holding his gun tightly. He slipped around a big boulder, peering into the foam for Arvada.

Suddenly it was a big, top-heavy figure looming up on a bathtub rock, and a gun flaming right in Manton's eyes. He felt the stunning pain of lead rocking into his hand, saw his Navy jump from smashed fingers. Arvada threw down again, a baleful, triumphant grin splitting his dark face. In that instant, Manton faced his death with only the thought of a yellow-haired woman.

Then he saw the smile fade from Arvada's face. The Creole thumbed angrily at his gun, snapping the hammer once, twice. It was empty. He threw it aside with a shrug, and that grin spread again. He jumped lightly from the bathtub rock and moved forward with that oddly graceful walk, juggling his weight back and forth, torso bending forward a little from the waist.

Savate!

Arvada was bigger and taller than Manton, broader and heavier — yet he moved with such an appalling ease that he might have been a lightweight. Manton felt suddenly awkward and helpless before the Creole. He had fought rough-and-tumble on the docks at St. Louis before he took to the cards, but he had never been skillful. He was strong enough, and the trek from the Missouri had put a steel edge to his strength. But what good was that? Mackinaw had been strong. Mackinaw, who snapped rifles like toothpicks, who threw men around like rubber balls, Mackinaw who took six slugs in his body without going down and still had crushed Clew Butler like a rag doll — Manton had never seen a stronger man. Yet Arvada had stopped the giant, all alone. Arvada had beaten him utterly.

Fighting with the feet like the *voyageurs* did, the rivermen. Arvada had been a riverman. He had been the master of all who fought that way on the wild Missouri.

Savate!

Manton knew there would be no point in sparring, and he made his forward lunge look as awkward and ill-timed as possible, sticking his chin out to form a target that Arvada couldn't resist. The Creole juggled over onto one foot, and his right boot came up at Manton, big, black, vicious. Manton threw himself aside, grabbing that boot, letting himself go on over. Arvada spun like a top, and went on his face. With amazing speed, he bounced erect.

But Manton had regained his feet, too, and he hit Arvada before the man had gained his balance. They went down again, smashing up against the bathtub rock. Manton hooked a right into Arvada's face, got a thumb punched in his eye for return. Then the Creole had slithered from beneath him.

Blinded in one eye, Manton got to his feet, turned to meet Arvada's rush. He couldn't see well enough, and he didn't catch the other's movement in time. A boot smashed into his mouth. Spitting blood and teeth, he went over on his back.

Manton had seen the thing happen to Mackinaw, and, when he caught sight of Arvada jumping for him, he fought his desire to roll, knowing it would be suicide. But the instinct to get his face out from under those biting caulks was too much, and he found himself spinning over onto his belly. Arvada hit him on the back of his neck, riding him as he would birl a log. Manton felt the caulks sink into his neck and shoulder, and he couldn't stop the scream of agony that burst from him. Still unable to halt his roll, he felt the crushing pair of those boots hit him in the side of the head. Arvada's next jump would catch him full in the face, just as it had Mackinaw.

With a terrible, spasmodic effort of will, Manton stopped rolling and jerked back, face down. Arvada's boots hit him on the back again. He heaved up under the agonizing bite of steel. Arvada tried to ride him down again, but Manton was on his hands and knees, and he came on up, forcing the Creole to dance off. The big gambler tried to whirl, but already Arvada was coming back in, giving him no time to set himself.

A boot caught Manton on his shoulder, and he staggered backward. Another caught him in the pit of his stomach as he turned, doubling him over. A third hit the side of his head, straightening him, forcing him to stumble on back to keep from falling.

Pain roared through his head; then a

greater roaring filled his consciousness. He felt the dampness of spray on his bloody neck, and suddenly realized that the Creole was methodically forcing him back toward the edge of the gorge so he could literally kick him off into a thousand feet of empty space.

He tried to dodge the next kick, but it caught him in the neck, and he collapsed to his hands and knees. One knee slipped over the smooth wet lava that formed the lip of the Snake's gorge. The next boot would put him into that gorge, and he saw it coming.

With a shuddering breath, he threw himself at Arvada, diving under the kick. Arvada had to dance forward to keep from falling because he had missed. Manton lit on his hands and knees, and the Creole went past him, already juggling for the follow-up.

But in that instant their positions were reversed. Arvada was now on the edge where Manton had stood before. He was spinning on one leg to deliver his kick.

Manton whirled from where he was on his hands and knees, and launched himself with an explosion of despairing strength that came from knowing this was his last bid. It threw the Creole's timing off, and his boot missed. His foot was still in the air when Manton's big body hurtled under it and smashed into his pivot leg. It was like toppling a ninepin.

One moment Manton was crashing into Arvada, with the harsh feel of the man's tree-trunk thigh against him. The next moment there was nothing. Arvada might have screamed as he went over backward into the greenish hell of the Snake River Gorge. Manton would never know. The all-enveloping roar of the falls was all he could hear, and he sagged down on the lip of lava, head dangling over, spent.

It seemed an eternity later that Owhee and Sol Lewis came running through the cloud of foam, rounding the bathtub rock. With them was Leah, and some of the other emigrants. Manton had dragged himself away from the edge and was lying with his head toward the trail, waiting for them. He didn't have the strength to rise. He caught the horror in the woman's eyes as she saw what a mess Arvada had made of his face. Then the horror changed to a deep compassion, and she ran toward him, calling something. He couldn't hear her. It didn't matter. She was kneeling beside him.

If Owhee was down here, that meant he and Lewis and the others had finished with Arvada's men, and it was all over. The sudden relief swept through Manton, and he laughed almost hysterically. Leah's eyes were wet with tears, but he could see the sudden happiness shine through them as she saw he was laughing. Sure, laughing. *I can laugh like other men, Leah. I can laugh and cry and hate and love and get mad and fight for what I want.* His laughter grew, shaking him, hurting him. He didn't care. It had been a long time coming. But now he was a human being again. He sagged back, choking out the words.

"When we get . . . to Grande Ronde . . . will you let me build that house for you, Leah?"

Her eyes were wide, puzzled.

He suddenly realized she couldn't hear him because of the roaring water. He could see her lips moving, probably asking him what he'd said. He didn't try to repeat it. There was no strength left in him for that. Besides, he knew, somehow, that she would let him build that house, and that, when it was finished, it would be their house.

Brand of Penasco:

A <u>Señorita</u> Scorpion Story

Les Savage, Jr., narrated the adventures of Elgera Douglas, better known as *Señorita Scorpion*, in a series of seven short novels appearing originally in *Action Stories*, a Fiction House magazine. She was by far the most popular literary series character to appear in the magazine in the nearly thirty years of its publication history. The first three short novels in the saga of Elgera Douglas are to be found in *The Legend of* Señorita *Scorpion* (Circle V Westerns, 1996). The fourth short novel about her, "The Curse of Montezuma," is collected in *The Return of* Señorita *Scorpion: A Western Trio* (Circle V Westerns, 1997), and the sixth appears in *The Lash of* Señorita *Scorpion: A Western Trio* (Circle V Westerns, 1998). This, the fifth short novel in the saga, was titled by the author "Brand of Penasco" and was sold to Fiction House on April 21, 1945, appearing under the title "Brand of the Gallows-Ghost" in *Action Stories* (Winter, 1945). The author was paid $375.00 for it upon acceptance, at the rate of

2½ ¢ a word. In the earlier installments in the saga, although both Chisos Owens and Johnny Hagar fall in love with Elgera, these romances are never consummated. In "The Lash of *Señorita* Scorpion" it seemed for a time that Elgera would succumb to the blandishments of the narrator of that short novel, U.S. Marshal Powder Welles, but this did not happen. For its first appearance since original magazine publication, the text and title of "Brand of Penasco" have been restored according to the author's typescript.

One 🐎

It was some nameless little Mexican town on the border. Sleeping adobe hovels threw lazy shadows across the dusty ruts of the wagon road that passed for the main street. Men reacted the same way men would have reacted in any town from the Río Grande to the Red River. A short, squat *peon* in shiny *mitaja* leggings came out of a shop advertised on a dirty sign as **Tienda de Másomenos**. The *peon* was halfway across the street before he stopped, turning slightly as he stared. Elgera Douglas licked her dry, cracked lips and kept right on walking up the middle of the street, limping painfully now because she had come a long way on high heels.

The *peon* said something softly, and another man came out of the *tienda,* carrying his sizable paunch in a red sash so broad it hid the bottom half of his wide shirt and the upper half of his dirty pantaloons. The fat man leaned forward and squinted.

"*Sacramento,*" he said. "*Señorita* Scorpion!"

The *peon* stiffened suddenly, and then

turned to run on across the street and into the adobe *cantina* called **Cueva de Cojo**. The door shut behind him with a hollow bang, raising echoes along the adobe walls, and then the echoes died, and for a moment Elgera was walking in silence once more. She had known it would be something like this, and she was breathing a little harder now, and it wasn't from the hike. Then, through the physical weight of the afternoon heat, it was other sounds, closing in around her. She turned to see a pair of young *vaqueros* in tattered *serapes* moving through the shadows on the east side of the street, moving parallel with her. One of them was fingering the rusty old Remington in his belt. Someone was behind her, too. She could hear his boots scraping the earth. As she neared the fat man in the red sash, he began to back up with little, mincing steps. Then another man was stepping out of the *tienda*.

Perhaps the first thing was the size of his head. He was over six feet tall, and carried his shoulders in an arrogant swagger that displayed their singular breadth, and his neck was like a muscular brown tree trunk, and still his head looked too large. His thick black hair fell long down his back, as some of the Indians still wore it in these archaic communities, and Elgera Douglas realized he must be a full-blooded Indian of Mexico, a Quill. He wore a short leather *charro* jacket that might have covered half the huge barrel of his torso, flapping open in front to reveal the network of scars patterning the heavy muscles of his chest and belly.

"Ah, *señorita*," he said thickly, and she saw how bloodshot his eyes were, "am I lost in the bibulous dreams of peyote, or do I really see a white woman coming down the street of our blessed *pueblo?*"

The fat man tried to catch him by the arm. "Bighead, don't be a *pendejo* . . . don't be a fool. Can't you see who it is . . . ? Don't you . . . ?"

"Másomenos," said Bighead, yanking away from the other, "all I see is a gorgeous creature with hair as blonde as a palomino's mane and lips as red as nopal after a spring rain, and eyes so blue I think I'm looking at heaven on a clear day. Isn't that what you see?"

"*Más o menos,*" shrugged the fat man, "more or less. *Pues.* . . ."

"*Pues nada,*" said Bighead, and lurched toward Elgera, "but nothing. If you see what I see, then it must be real. And look at the way those *charro* pants fit her. So tight all those roses sewn down the seams would pop off if she bent over."

Elgera had stopped, standing there with the spike heels of her basket-stamped Hyers spread wide in the street. "Up where I come from a man doesn't talk that way to a lady. You hadn't better come any closer."

Maybe it was the tone of her voice that stopped him, or the flash in her eye. He straightened up slightly, one big hand still held out in front of him, and she could mark the subtle degeneracy drawing its deep lines in his heavy-fleshed face. Without having to see it, she knew the other men closed in around her, and a constriction was growing in her chest. Bighead laughed suddenly.

"Ah, a *gata*," he said, "a wildcat, too. And just where do you come from? It isn't every *día* a white woman comes walking into our *pueblo* alone."

"Maybe I came to see a man about a horse," she said.

Másomenas grabbed Bighead again. "Please, Bighead, you don't know who she is. Let El Cojo handle this. Tico went to get him."

"*Basta*," shouted Bighead, throwing out the arm Másomenos held in a sudden violent gesture, "I'll handle anything The Lame One can." The thrust hurled the gross man in the red sash back against the wall so hard his legs went out from under him, and the *ristras* of red chiles were knocked from their *viga* pole above to drape themselves around his fat neck where he sat on the ground. "You want to see a man about a *caballo, rosa mía?*" Bighead shouted at Elgera, lurching toward her again. "I'll show you *caballos*. I'll show you all the horses in *Méjico*."

She heard the scuffling movement of the men around her spreading away, and her thick, tawny brows arched in a sudden wild way as she leaned forward a little, but otherwise she did not move. "Don't put your hands on me, Bighead!"

He laughed uproaringly, and the fetid odor of his unwashed body swept her as he took the last step that brought him close enough to grab her, and his huge hands fell, hot and heavy, against her shoulders. Elgera's whole body stiffened, but whatever she would have done was circumvented by the sibilant words from behind Bighead.

"That will do, Bighead. Take your hands off."

Bighead's hands tightened on her shoulders with such a terrible grip that she almost cried out with the pain, but there was something spasmodic about it that held her from any action. He stood there, towering above her, and then something crossed his dissipated face, and his hands relaxed, and he stepped back.

The man behind Bighead was dwarfed by the giant Quill without actually seeming small. His lean, dark face was filled with a brooding, mordant intelligence, and his black eyes, meeting Elgera's, seemed to glow with some inner fever. He wore his abundance of black hair in a queue that seemed incongruous with his faultlessly tailored blue cutaway and pin-striped trousers. His thin lips moved over his white teeth in a careful, deliberate enunciation that hinted at his foreign origin, although the words held no discernible accent.

"This *pueblo* was an unfortunate choice for your visit, *señorita,* but let me extend a welcome anyway. You are standing on the main *calle* of Oro Peso, and, if you want a horse, you had better discuss it with me, because I am El Cojo, and I own Oro Peso."

The inside of the Cueva de Cojo belied the dilapidated exterior. A gleaming mahogany bar stretched the twenty-foot length of one wall, an expensive, gold-framed mirror as long as the bar hanging over the shelves of bottles, portraits of Santa Anna and Porfirio Díaz suspended regally above the mirror. There was a faro layout and a roulette wheel on the other side, toward the rear, and a scattering of heavy mahogany deal tables near the windowless front wall. Elgera had never known a lean bartender, and this one was as short and square as the bottle of Kentucky he was polishing, and he had a gotched ear that only added to the ugly iniquity of his face. The *peon* in the shiny *mitaja* leggings who had come in to get El Cojo was standing near the door with several other seedy-looking customers in dirty white pantaloons, and they watched Elgera all the way back to the rear door that led into a sumptuous office. El Cojo closed the heavy brass-bound portal softly, motioning toward an overstuffed Queen Anne to one side of the ponderous hand-carved *escritorio*. She ignored the armchair, taking a breath of the faint odor of expensive whiskey before she spoke.

"What's wrong with your town, anyway? It looks like an armed camp."

El Cojo shrugged, limping to the hand-carved desk, placing his thumb and forefinger on the edges of the lid to an ebony box and opening it. "If you won't sit down, at least have a *cigarillo*. I smoke cheroots myself, but these come from Mexico City. As Bighead told you, it is not often a woman comes. . . ."

"It was more than that. They were like a bunch of dogs ready to jump a cat."

His thin lips formed a faint, ironic smile as she shook her head at the cigarettes. "I have heard that *Señorita* Scorpion always has a singular effect on men."

"You know it wasn't that."

He shrugged tailored shoulders. "Very well. I told you this was an unfortunate town for a visit. You come from the Big Bend. You must have heard it up there. It is said that Penasco is riding again."

She made an impatient gesture with her hand. "The *Rurales* hung him in 'Eighty-One."

"Did you see the dead body?"

"Of course not."

"I have never met anyone who has." He ran a finger across his black hair. "He is almost a legendary figure now. Many stories have grown up around him. Some say he escaped the *Rurales,* so wounded that he would never sit on a horse again . . . escaped into the Chisos Mountains. Others say his spirit has returned to ride his giant black horse, El Morzillo, once more when the moon is full."

She took a weary breath. "Those stories have been in circulation for ten years, just like the ones about Billy the Kid. I've never seen a border town affected by them like this."

"But it is no longer stories." El Cojo poured a drink from a cut-glass decanter, but she waved it away. His ironic smile grew. "A month or so ago Parque Guerrera, a big *ranchero* near Castellán, north of the Río, was found murdered in the road, and on his cheek was stamped the *Rúbrica de Penasco.*"

She drew in her breath. "The Brand of Penasco?"

"Yes," he smiled. "You know the story. Penasco was descended from the ancient Moorish family in Spain whose brand was called a *rúbrica*. This *rúbrica* was inscribed in a ring, and they sealed their letters with it instead of signing their name, pressing the seal into hot wax and stamping it onto the paper. They also used it to brand their possessions, and the ring was handed down from eldest son to eldest son, passing from Spain to Mexico when Real Penasco's grandfather came to the New World, eventually coming to Real himself. The House of Penasco had the misfortune to sympathize with Maximilian when the French sent him to rule Mexico, and, when Juárez overthrew Maximilian, the estate of the Penascos was confiscated by the new government in a rather bloody manner which left only Real alive. He was about fourteen, and he fled to the hills and swore vengeance on all those responsible for the death of his family and the ruin of his house." Cojo sipped at the drink, studying her with those glowing eyes, and she sensed something behind his easy talk. "It has come out that this Guerrera who was murdered near Castellán once held a high position under Juárez. Does that explain the tension in our little *pueblo?*"

"Does it?" she said.

He shrugged, as if he had done all he could. "*Pues, señorita,* there are still many hereabouts who were loyal supporters of Juárez. You can understand their apprehension, if Penasco is abroad. I, for one, would not want to be on his list. Why did you come to Oro Peso?"

The abrupt change took her off guard, and he must have seen it because he laughed softly, and she realized it was what he had intended. "I . . ." — she hesitated, then, wondering if it would be a mistake to tell him what she had really been doing this near the border. Wide-eyed she met his glance. "I was coming back from buying cattle at Santa Helena. I lost my horse somewhere near Castellán."

"*Buying* cattle . . . at the border." The way he said it held a disbelief, but his shrug was an acceptance. "I'm surprised such a rider as you let her horse escape her."

"I was in a hurry and took a short cut ahead of my crew. Got off to water my horse crossing the Río. Sidewinder must have spooked it. I've been footing it most of the day now, and Oro Peso's the first place I hit, and I'd like to get another horse. I'll sign your check or leave an I.O.U., anything you like."

"Ah," — his surprised look didn't convince her, somehow — "you have no money."

"You know me here. You know I'll be good for it."

"We know of you, *señorita*. The Scorpion? I don't wonder they call you that. I wager you would have bitten Bighead in another moment, if I hadn't come out there, and I fully believe he would have died of the bite." His smile was deprecating. "Yes, we know of you. But the things that have come to our ears are hardly a bond for the price of a horse."

She flushed. "Perhaps I'd better see someone else."

"Who?" He toyed with his cheroot. "No one would sell you a horse in this town without my permission" — she had made a move to the door, and he held out his hand, tilting his head to one side — "and if you are thinking of another way, I would advise against it. They treat a horse thief the same way here as they do in Texas, whether they're man or woman."

"But I'm stranded here."

"There are other forms of payment." He caught the flash in her eye, and waved it away with his hand. "Don't misunderstand me. What I mean is . . . I have a nice little place here where all the *vaqueros* from miles around like to gather. I have a Mexican dancer for attraction, and good liquor, but my house gamblers are all inferior *hombres*. I myself have some skill with cards, but I can't spend much time at the tables. Now, if I had a faro banker, for instance, who had never been known to lose at the game, and who provided the added attraction of being one of the most beautiful and famous women in Texas, I'll lay you deuces to aces we'd have *vaqueros* coming up here from as far south as Mexico City."

"Don't be a fool!"

She saw the blood rise to his dark face, and it was a long moment before his voice came, hardly audible at first. "Few have called me a fool with impunity, *señorita*." He waited a moment, studying her, then went on carefully. "I am a businessman, making you a generous proposition. If you banked my faro game for one week, I would make more money than I do at present in six months. As you say, we've heard of you. I guess there isn't a horse made you can't ride, is there? Or a gun holstered you can't get out quicker than any man in Texas? Or a deck of cards you can't turn into four aces every hand?"

"I never touched a marked card. . . ."

"I never marked a card." He smiled suddenly. "Perhaps that is why I don't make money off my layouts. At any rate, you would be playing a straight game. Faro, chusa, poker, whatever you chose. Do it for a week and I'll give you a horse that would even outmatch that palomino of yours."

She wondered why he really wanted her to stay. "You'd put your house behind me in a straight game?"

"And still win every hand. *Si*." He eyed her shrewdly. "Or are you afraid . . . with men coming in from so far to play at your table . . . are you afraid you would finally meet someone who could win your hand?"

She stiffened, and her long blonde hair caught a ripple of light as she tossed her head. "I'll accept your proposition."

"I thought that would touch your gambler's spirit. Never afraid to take a chance with the cards, eh, or a horse . . . or a gun?"

He limped to open the door, ushering her out. "Now you must want to clean up after that long walk. I will have the best meal in all the border waiting when you're ready. I'm sure you won't mind sharing Lupita's room. She's the dancer I mentioned. Out . . . just now . . . but you'll meet her this evening."

The door behind the bar opened on a narrow hall that led between cool brown adobe walls to chambers behind El Cojo's office. Lupita's quarters were small but reflected the same surprising sumptuousness as the office, a Brussels carpet replacing the usual Navajo rugs found in border houses, a huge double bedstead of mahogany with a Louis Seize curved top inlaid with *tuya* wood.

"You'll find a second bed in the other room, and I'll have my Indian bring in a big tub of warm water if you want to wash all over," said The Lame One. He stopped a moment at the door, meeting her eyes, and then, with that faint, sardonic smile, turned and left. She tested the bed, sinking into the rich damask coverlet, and then rose with a grimace. There was something voluptuous about the whole room that left a bad taste in her mouth.

"Perhaps you are more used to the hard

leather of a saddle, *señorita*."

Bighead stood in the doorway leading to the second room, swaying slightly, the tight leather vest pulled open across the front still revealing the pattern of scars across his thickly-muscled torso. She stood rigidly by the bed, only realizing she had grabbed one of the carved posts when her hand began to ache with the force of her grip. She relaxed slightly.

"I was waiting for Lupita," said Bighead, moving unsteadily into the room. "But I think I like you better. You are staying with us a while?"

"You're drunk!"

"I usually am. It makes life so much happier that way. What do you say we finish what I started out in the street?"

"You aren't finishing anything," Elgera said tensely, and the damask whispered against her *charro* leggings as she slid down the side of the bed toward the kneehole dressing table. "You'd better get out, Bighead. You'd better not try to put your hands on me again."

"*Sacramento*," he laughed, catching at the bedpost as he lurched around the foot toward her, "*Señorita* Scorpion in all her glory. I like a wildcat. Fight me all you want, *sancha múa*, it makes me want you that much more."

He stumbled forward, big hands reaching for her. She had it in her fist now. It was a heavy, long-necked perfume bottle of cut-glass, and it made a dull, cracking sound against his head.

"*¡Madre de Dios!*" he screamed, and the bed gave beneath his ponderous weight falling over onto it. He struggled to get back on his feet, sinking his hands into the damask as if for help, grunting like a wounded animal. Even through his pain, he must have heard the crash of glass. He turned his head slightly, still against the coverlet, and saw her standing there with the broken bottle in her hand. She had knocked the bottom off against the table, spilling the perfume in an amber flood over her *charro* trousers and the chintz hangings of the dresser. In the cloying scent that filled the room, he pushed himself off the bed, clutching for the post again to keep from falling as he backed away.

"No . . ." — he held out his hand, pawing at the air — "*¡Dios, no . . . Madre de Dios . . . !*"

"Then get out," she said bitterly, holding the broken end of the bottle toward him. "Get out, or I'll put this in your face."

Still dazed from the blow, he lurched backward, grabbing wildly for the door handle. He jerked the heavy portal farther open, and then braced himself against the frame that last moment, shaking his head. "All right. All right. But this doesn't end it. You'll be sorry you came here. I'm not talking about me now. I'll get you sometime when there aren't any glass bottles, or any El Cojo. But I'm not even talking about that now. You don't know what you stepped into here at Oro Peso. You wanted a horse? You're on one right now. You got on one the minute you hit this town. It only goes one way, and that's straight to hell, and it don't ever come back!"

 # Two

The wind whined mordantly out of the Chisos Mountains to rattle through the pipe-stem cactus here in the basin south of the footslopes and raise a haze of alkali that turned the mesquite into a ghostly pattern of clawing fingers against the faint illumination of the moon. The big dun mare leaned against the blowing force with head down, and Chisos Owens hunched forward in the heavy Porter saddle, one rope-scarred hand holding a tattered bandanna across his nose and mouth to shield him from the acrid dust. He was watching his horse for some sign, because animals could usually sense a presence quicker than a man, and he had his own head cocked at the same time, listening for it again. Finally he stepped out of the big roping rig and dropped the rawhide reins over his horse's head. Then he turned to pull his six-teen-shot Henry from the saddle scabbard.

"Leave the rifle where it is, *señor*, if you please." Chisos stiffened to the sibilant voice coming somewhere from the mesquite, then dropped his hand off the

Henry's battered butt. "And step away from the *caballo* and very carefully pull out your revolver and drop it."

Chisos complied, and then turned slightly to the rattle of the brush as the men moved into the open. One of them was tall and heavy-shouldered in a gaudy *charro* coat trimmed with gilt and a tremendous glazed sombrero heavy with silver embroidery, moving in a bow-legged, saddle-bound walk that swung his upper body from side to side and kept the fancy serape flapping at the empty holster thonged down around his tight buckskin *chivarras*. He was shackled and stopped just free of the mesquite, and the second figure stepped around from behind him. This was the man with the gun. It loomed big in the man's sinewy hand, and Chisos Owens caught the dull gleam off his hair beneath his hat; it was as white as the alkali sifting up from beneath their feet.

"You must be pretty spooky, Zaragosa," said Chisos. "Hide that way every time a hossbacker bulges out?"

The white-haired man came closer, lean and straight as a whipstock in the dark military uniform of the *Rurales*. He peered at Chisos, and the drawn, haggard lines of his face accentuated its apparent age.

"Chisos Owens!" he said, reaching out to

145

grip Chisos's hand. "I might have known it. Who else would ride alone these nights. Forgive me, *amigo*, but an old fox gets to looking for a hound behind every bush, and in the darkness I did not recognize you. It has been too long since we shared the mescal together at your Smoky Blue *rancho*, eh?" He waved his Colt at the handcuffed man. "This is Tequila. I am escorting him to Durango for a bit of cattle appropriation he has been carrying on both above and below the border."

The other man laughed heartily. "*Sí*, it has been sort of a race between the Texas Rangers and the Mexican *Rurales* to see whose hospitality I would enjoy. In a way, I'm glad it has finally been decided."

"Don't be a hypocrite," said Captain Zaragosa. "You know you'd jump at the chance to shed those manacles. Our camp is deeper within the *mogotes, Señor* Chisos. You heard our horses whinny? That must have been when we decided to see who was out here. There is coffee on, if you'll join an old friend."

Chisos had been in the saddle all day, and he was glad enough to follow them through the thicket of mesquite and *agrito* to the small clearing where a fire crackled, hidden in a ditch formed by erosion. The captain looked at Chisos again, taking in the solid heft of his figure, almost as wide through the waist as the shoulders without any indication of fat.

"What are you doing this far south of your Chisos Mountains?"

Chisos had difficulty getting his mackinaw off the bulk of his shoulders. "Hunting Elgera Douglas."

"The one they call *Señorita* Scorpion?"

"I don't know why they ever tacked that on her," said Chisos, dropping his mackinaw and hunkering over the blaze.

"I understand it fits her," said Tequila. He sat cross-legged on the other side of the fire, and the flickering light cast his pockmarked face into blazing shadows, revealing a deep, gruesome gash across the bridge of his great, beaked nose.

"Oh, it fits her well enough," Chisos spat disgustedly, "but whoever heard of calling a girl that."

"There was Calamity Jane," said Zaragosa, pouring the coffee.

"All right, all right," shrugged Chisos, glancing at their unsaddled horses, picketed back in the brush. "You haven't seen a palomino around here these past few days, have you?"

"La Rubia?" said Tequila.

Chisos looked up at the man, his eyes tightening till a network of wrinkles spread away from them through the grime covering his face. "You saw it?"

"No," laughed Tequila, "but I guess everybody down here has heard just as much about the Scorpion's horse as they have about the Scorpion herself."

"Let's just call her Elgera Douglas," said Chisos wearily. He accepted the tin cup of coffee Zaragosa handed him. "You couldn't miss The Blonde if you saw it. Prettiest palomino in Texas. Hide like a gold piece just minted and a mane as blonde as Elgera's own hair, and so long it keeps her fetlocks clean."

"But why the horse?" said the captain.

"Some cattle were run off Elgera's Santiago spread last week, and she and her brother followed them as far as the Río Grande before they lost the trail," said Chisos. "They were hunting tracks across the Río, and the girl got separated from her brother in the dark. Come morning, he hunted around, but couldn't find her, and figured she had thought he had gone on back home. She wasn't at the Santiago when he got there. That was three days ago. I thought if her horse had thrown her, somebody might have spotted the animal,

148

even if they didn't see her."

"I didn't think she *could* be thrown," said Tequila.

Chisos shifted irritably, disliking the speculative gleam in the man's black eyes. He rubbed one big fist down his worn bat-wing chaps, looking from Tequila to the *Rurale*.

Zaragosa was frowning into the fire, tapping his cup with a lean brown finger. "I hate to say this," he muttered finally, "but it might as well be taken into consideration. The Penasco story has started again."

"I've heard that before," said Chisos.

"But this time it has some foundation," said the white-headed captain. "Parque Guerrera was found murdered on the road to Castellán sometime ago, his face stamped with the *Rúbrica de Penasco*."

Chisos reached for his mackinaw, feeling cold suddenly, and then he realized it wasn't the night. "You mean she . . . ?"

"Is it any less logical than to think *Señorita* Scorpion was thrown by her horse?" asked Captain Zaragosa.

"That's why you were so spooky," said Chisos.

"Penasco?" Zaragosa nodded, indicating his white hair. "Ordinary *hombres* have cause enough to be nervous when Penasco is abroad, but I have a sort of special reason.

I have been in the *Rurales* a long time, *Señor* Chisos. It was my dubious honor to command the men who captured Real Penasco in 'Eighty-One."

"Then you . . . of all people . . . should know whether he's dead or not."

The haggard lines of Zaragosa's face seemed to deepen. "Penasco was shot up pretty badly, many bullets in his legs and body, and we were afraid to try and reach Mexico City with him for fear his followers would effect his release as they had so many times before. Thus we took him to Manalca. I wired the capital for authority to hang him and got it. I saw Penasco hung, and I heard the doctor pronounce him dead. We could get none of the *peones* to dig the grave for us and had to do it ourselves. While we were thus engaged, the body disappeared from the *jacal* in which we had deposited it. The people say they saw him riding away on El Morzillo, his black horse. I thought at first he had been carried off by some of the *peones*. I could have sworn he was dead, and I had the doctor's testimony to back me up. Yet the doctor was a *peon*, and the *peones* were Penasco's friends." Zaragosa shook his head. "I don't know . . . I don't know."

Chisos was staring into the fire, and the story gave him a eerie feeling, somehow.

"This Penasco . . . at least you know what he looked like."

Zaragosa shrugged apologetically. "It may seem strange to you, *señor,* but I could not tell you what he looked like. It was night when we caught him, and we hung him before morning. We identified him by the guns he wore, the *Rúbrica de Penasco* carved into their ivory handles. No other man would have dared possess such weapons. We had fire light, but a man only gains impressions by that, and not the full appearance. . . ."

"Quit rationalizing, *Capitán,*" laughed Tequila. "You were a young scrub of a *cabo* so afraid of the *gato* you'd captured you didn't even stop to look at him good."

"*Sí,* we did rush him to Manalca as soon as we got the manacles on him," conceded Zaragosa. Then he turned to stare at his prisoner. "How did you know I was a corporal then?"

"I know you were a *cabo* then . . . I know you rode a sorrel gelding with a whey belly that dragged the ground when it walked," said Tequila. "I know many things, *Capitán.* Maybe even what Real Penasco looks like."

Zaragosa had stiffened. "You are a *pendejo.* Nobody really knows what he looked like. Not even those who were his friends."

"You mean nobody who knew ever told what he looks like," said Tequila. His grin tilted his eyes upward in a puckish, Oriental slyness. "What would you give me for an accurate description, *Capitán?*"

"You can't describe him any more than I can."

Tequila laughed. "He is a big man, *señores,* with shoulders like the *toros* they used to breed for the bullrings, and he is never without his short, blue *capuz.* He was in the smallpox epidemic at Hermosilla in 'Sixty-Seven, and he is badly marked about the face, and the saber of a *Rurale* almost severed his nose, leaving a deep, ugly gash across the bridge which. . . ."

"*¡Cállate la boca!*" shouted Zaragosa, leaping erect, "shut your trap!" He stood there, leaning toward Tequila, his fists clenched, lean body trembling perceptibly. Finally he turned to Chisos, the muscles contracted about his mouth till there was a deep, white groove on either side. He waved a frustrated hand at Tequila. "You see what I have to put up with all the time? He thinks it is his sense of humor."

Tequila threw his head back to laugh, and the firelight caught the gruesome pockmarks covering his face. Then he stopped laughing, and the grin that remained seemed to hold little mirth. "Perhaps I am not joking, Zaragosa. Did you ever think of that? I could be Penasco just as much as anybody else."

Zaragosa spat it out. "A coyote could be Penasco before you."

Tequila turned to Chisos, inclining his head toward the captain. "Zaragosa is rather touchy about Penasco, no? I would be, too, if I had been the one who had hung him."

"If you say anything more, I will give you a pistol-whipping that will remove any evidence of smallpox on your face," said Zaragosa venomously, and then turned to Chisos with some effort. "Are you spending the night here with us, *Señor* Chisos?"

He had not liked the sly look in Tequila's eyes. Chisos lay in his tattered, fetid sougan, thinking that. He had not liked the sly look. A hooty owl mourned softly somewhere in the footslopes beyond this stretch of brush, and a scud of clouds lazed across the moon's yellow face. In the new darkness cast by the clouds, Chisos shifted restlessly. He could hear Zaragosa breathing quietly across the fire. Then another sound impinged itself on his consciousness. He turned his head toward it carefully, light-colored hair falling tousled over his grimy brow, and his hand sought the Bisley .44 beneath the blankets. He relaxed abruptly, a wry smile catching at his strong lips. The horses. *Damn you, Chisos, getting as spooky as Zaragosa.*

He worked down into the blankets, reaching for sleep. Then it was Elgera, coming through the drowsiness that settled over him. She was never out of his mind, really. Sleeping or waking, the picture of her was always with him. He wondered how many other men felt that way about her. Every *hombre* from the Red River to Mexico City, they said. Yet, he felt it was different with him, somehow. Even her feeling for him was different than toward other men. That wry grin came once more. Every other man probably told himself the same thing.

Chisos drew taut again beneath his blankets. Not the horses this time. He turned his head so he could see where Tequila lay across the fire, his hands above his head, chained to the thick trunk of a mesquite by the manacles. The steady rise and fall of the man's breathing seemed natural enough. Chisos watched him a long time before he put his head back. Again it was Elgera, touching his mind with soft fingers, and finally he must have dozed.

At first he thought it was still in his sleep.

It was a sharp, thudding noise, and he took a heavy breath and rolled over in his sougan. Then he was wide awake, and turned so he could stare directly at the tall figure bent over *Capitán* Zaragosa's body. Chisos tried to haul himself from the blankets, pulling out his gun with a yank, but his body was still pinned in there when Tequila jumped him, manacled hands raised above his head. Chisos tried to roll away and get his gun out. The Mexican's body came down with a stunning weight, and all the air left Chisos in a sick grunt.

He had his gun free finally, twisting the heavy Bisley up. Tequila knocked it aside as it exploded, grabbing the weapon in both hands. Chisos yelled with the pain of a twisted wrist, but his big, rope-scarred fist was like a vise on the gun. Tequila yanked at it again, with no more success, and then, to stop Chisos from fighting out from beneath him, the Mexican released his grip on the gun and brought his manacled hands back over his head that way once more. Chisos knew what was coming, and tried to jerk aside, but the man was straddling him, pinning him down, and he was helpless to escape it. He managed to pull his gun in line again, and squeeze the trigger, and the roar of the shot was simultaneous with the crashing agony of those heavy manacles coming down across his face.

Chisos heard someone groaning and realized it was himself, and there were other dim, unreal sounds coming through the pain. Finally, after what seemed an eternity, he felt full consciousness returning. He managed to sit up, and it caused him more pain to shake his head. The Bisley was still gripped in one fist. He pawed at his face and felt the mashed flesh, and his hand came away covered with thick, viscous blood.

"Chisos," mumbled Zaragosa, trying to gain his feet over there. His face was bloody, too, and Chisos realized Tequila must have knocked him out the same way. "I had him chained to that mesquite. The devil dug it out . . . roots and all."

Chisos remembered then the sounds he had heard, and saw the uprooted bush, and the hole where it had stood in the sandy loam. Finally the big man got to his own feet and stumbled over to where the horses had stood. He found the marks leading into the mesquite and plunged after them.

"Don't be a *pendejo*," cried Zaragosa, coming after him, "don't be a fool. You can't catch him on horseback."

"If he's riding my dun, he won't be able to

drive it far!" shouted Chisos hoarsely. "It's a smart hoss, and it'll break free of him as soon as it gets the chance. I'll be there when it does."

It was heavy going in his high-heeled boots, and his head was swimming with pain from the blow. Bisley gripped in his tense fist, he followed the trail through the brush, sometimes by the hoof marks in the soft ground, sometimes by the holes ripped in the thick *mogotes* by the horses passing through. His chest was heaving, and he had lost all passage of time when he came across the dun. It was grazing on some curly red mesquite grass, and it shied away from him as soon as he broke into the open.

"Diablo," called Chisos angrily, but the horse continued to back away, watching him cunningly. He snaked off his belt, and again started forward. The horse turned broadside to him as it whirled to dance away, and he threw the belt. It fell across the dun's broad back. The animal halted, even though the belt slid off, and remained standing there till Chisos reached it. He was using his belt and bandanna to knot a hackamore around the dun's lower jaw as Zaragosa came up.

"*Sacramento,*" panted the captain. "You have the smart *caballo*."

"He thought the belt was my rope," said Chisos. "Must have been trained to the rope by some hand who hadn't ever heard about gentling a horse. Diablo's so skeery of the clothesline you don't have to put your loop on him. Throw the string across his back, and he's yours. Now, how about Tequila?"

He had finished the hackamore and was about to mount, when Zaragosa caught his arm with a hissing, indrawn breath. Chisos turned to look where the captain was pointing with his other trembling hand. They were standing in the last cluster of mesquite before the rising footslopes of the Chisos Mountains. The clouds had swept past the moon now, and in the new light the man was plain enough, sitting his horse on the first crest.

"El Morzillo," said Zaragosa in a hushed voice. "Penasco!"

"You're loco," Chisos told him sharply, "that's Tequila on your black nag. . . ."

"No" — Zaragosa tore free as Chisos tried to grab him — "no." His face held a pale terror. *No!* and he crashed away from Chisos into the brush like a frenzied animal.

"Zaragosa!" Chisos whirled to his animal, the hackamore in one hand, his other hand slapping onto its withers as he jumped up, scissoring his legs over its back, turning the horse after the captain. The animal had some steel dust in its blocky quarters, and, when he let it out like this, it got its cold mouth on the bit, and he had all he could do to keep the horse from running itself to death. Now, with only the hackamore for control, it was a constant battle through the brush, and he had lost the captain within a few hundred yards. He finally managed to haul the dun down, dismounting to head it back and find the trail again.

"You're a good hoss," he told Diablo under his breath, "but I wish to hell you wouldn't try and run away from me every time I get on your back."

He found the place they had started from and hunted for some mark that would put him on the trail again, but he had made such a mess, popping through the brush after Zaragosa, that any decent sign had been obliterated. He stared at the ridge again, rising black and empty now, beneath the moon. The shot startled him, coming clear on the night air. It was not far away, and he found a dense thicket and tied the horse in there with the hackamore. Then he began making his way toward the ridge. It had come from up there somewhere. He was still in the mesquite when he found where Zaragosa had gone.

Chisos hunkered down with his gun out, breathing silently. He stayed there a long time, raking the far brush with his glance, listening. Then he began to circle the clearing, slowly, patiently, stopping to listen and look every few feet. He had completed the circle within half an hour. Finally he moved out into the open and squatted down beside Zaragosa's body. The bullet hole was faintly visible in the blood that had leaked out across his chest, and the fear was still stamped in the gaunt *Rurale*'s face. But there was something else stamped there. Chisos bent closer, squinting at the man's right cheek to make sure, and his blunt finger traced the design on the skin, and finally his lips formed the words without sound. *La Rúbrica de Penasco.* The Brand of Penasco.

Three 🐎

Lupita Tovar's face had been pitted deeply with smallpox. She had a husky, rasping voice, and Elgera Douglas found herself wondering why El Cojo had ever chosen the girl for an entertainer. Lupita stood at the foot of the heavy Louis Seize bed, a black velvet basque tightly laced down the slim line of her body, a red silk skirt flaring out beneath, with a dark petticoat showing under that. She had been watching Elgera pin a scarlet rose in her blonde hair, preparatory to taking over her faro table outside.

"You will look very beautiful to El Cojo this evening, *Señorita* Scorpion." The way she said the name made Elgera turn from the kneehole dressing table. "What do you think of The Lame One by now?"

Elgera smiled faintly, studying the other woman's pocked face. "El Cojo is a strange person. So unlike any man I've known before."

"He is a gentleman."

"Oh." Elgera nodded, pursing her lips.

Lupita bent forward slightly, and her big

161

black eyes were the only attractive thing about her face, and a new intensity had entered them. "You will leave, won't you? When this agreement between you and Cojo is over, you'll take the horse he gives you and leave."

"I'm borrowing your perfume again." Elgera had turned back to the dresser, lifting the glass stopper out of the new bottle to touch her hair. Her voice became sober. "Don't worry about Cojo. Everything will be all right."

Lupita's skirt whispered sibilantly behind Elgera, and the movement had brought the Mexican girl around beside the dresser. "Don't try to tell me that. I've seen the way Cojo looks at you. I know what you are, Señorita Scorpion" — she almost spat it out this time, and her small bosom was rising and falling more rapidly — "I've heard all about you."

"I can't help how he looks at me," Elgera said.

"You'll go." Lupita's veined hand was on the edge of the dresser, gripping it till the bones gleamed whitely through the dark flesh. "You'll go, or you'll wish you never saw Oro Peso."

Elgera turned to study her face. "Do you want me to leave just because of Cojo . . .

or something else?"

Lupita lifted her hand off the dresser in an involuntary way and looked as if she were going to step back. Then she seemed to recover herself. "What do you mean?"

"Yes," said El Cojo from the doorway, "what do you mean?"

Both women turned toward him sharply, and he limped in, that soft, ironic smile revealing his teeth in a faintly shadowed line, his strange, glowing eyes settling on Elgera. He waved a ringed hand at Lupita.

"It is time for your number, *sancha múa*."

"Cojo. . . ."

"I said it is time for your number." He had not raised his voice, but the velvet tone had grown more intense. Elgera saw the perceptible diminution of color in Lupita's pocked cheeks. Then the Mexican dancer bit her underlip, and her skirts hissed past Cojo. He went over to the bed, running his sensitive fingers delicately over the gilt tracery on the post, waiting till Lupita was gone.

"Don't mind her," he said. "Naturally, she's jealous. She's the daughter of old friends, and I gave her the job out of . . ." — he shrugged, motioning vaguely toward his face — "you know."

"Are you sure that's all, Cojo. There isn't more?"

His surprise was just mild enough. "How do you mean?"

"You know." She had turned back to the mirror, but he could see her face reflected in the glass, and the faint smile.

He laughed abruptly, as if it had just come to him, and shrugged that way again. "Well, perhaps Lupita is a bit impetuous. A racial attribute. . . ."

"All I mean is, I don't think Lupita would take it passively when she discovered someone else she thought had been dealing from the top was really pulling the cards off the bottom."

"When you first came here," he said, "I told you this house backed a straight game. Whatever Lupita gave you to believe lies between her and myself is strictly her own interpretation."

Elgera turned to study his face, and, oddly enough, she believed him now. There was something sardonic in its narrow, satanic caste, but there was something brooding, too, something almost sad, and it touched her. "You're a strange man, Cojo."

"You mean because I am the only one who has not made advances toward you?" he asked, unsmiling.

At first, she took this for egotism and turned back to the mirror with an impatient toss of her head, anger replacing other emotion. Then she realized it wasn't the egotism that angered her, but the fact that he had struck home. She smiled abruptly at him in the mirror despite herself, and he returned the smile faintly.

"Perhaps I have a different approach," he said.

"Perhaps you made a mistake in telling me."

"Did I?" The inveterate gambler, he always had a pack of cards, and they were in his hands now. "I will cut you for a kiss. High card wins."

The abruptness of that caught her off guard. "I'm rather disappointed in you," she said.

"Perhaps it is not as crude as it appears," he said. "Are you afraid?"

"I won't dignify that with an answer."

"Oh." He studied the cards, a soft smile playing about his strong, thin lips. "I had heard you were a gambler. Horses, men, cards . . . it did not matter. But I guess you're just a woman, after all."

Her blonde hair rippled with the toss of her head, and her voice had a tight, goaded sound. "Shuffle them."

His laugh was sibilant. "Was it so crude now?" He shuffled the cards, held them out to her. "Cut?"

Again she could not help smiling. Tucking her lower lip beneath her teeth, she cut the deck. She had a momentary impulse to run her finger along the top edge for nail marks and then looked up at him, and was sorry for it, somehow. He let her draw first. She turned a king of spades face up on the dresser. He licked his slender forefinger and turned a four of clubs.

"How unfortunate. Perhaps the next time, no?" His laugh was easy, then he dismissed it with a shrug, inclining his dark head toward the door. "I imagine the gentlemen at the faro layout are getting impatient."

She moved after him, wondering if that was all it had meant to him. "You say I'm a gambler, Cojo, yet you put me at a faro layout."

The smoky sounds from the other room swept against her as he opened the door. "What's wrong with the faro layout?"

"All I do is sit and deal. . . ."

"That's it. Poker . . . you'd get the deal once out of every four or five times. Faro . . . the cards are in the house's hands all the time. The mathematical probabilities are with us that way. My games are straight, but I've got to make some profit. What's wrong with faro, anyway? You have a fifty-fifty chance. What gambler could ask better odds?"

"There's a little skill connected with poker," she said petulantly.

That seemed to amuse him, and he started to laugh softly, when a shuffling sound in the hall behind turned them toward the rear door, leading into the rear alley. Lupita was drawing a tall man in a huge sombrero into the short hallway, his broad shoulders towering over her dark head. She saw Elgera and Cojo and kept turned halfway toward the man behind her, holding her hands down in a strange, stiff way so that her flaring skirt blocked off the lower part of his body.

"Cojo," she said. "Cojo. . . ."

Cojo took a look at the man's face, glanced at Elgera, then back again at the others. "All right, all right . . . in my office," he said swiftly, and waved his hand absently at Elgera. "You go on. I'll be out in a minute."

Before she left the end of the hall, Elgera looked back once more. Cojo was almost to the office door, and Lupita was pushing the tall man through. Light from outside the office fell across his face, covered with smallpox scars, the great, beaked nose gashed gruesomely across its bridge from some old wound. And in that moment, his hands were out in front of him, not hidden by Lupita's skirts. They were manacled.

Elgera moved into the front saloon slowly, a speculative frown drawing her tawny brows together. Then she forgot about the handcuffed man. There was another man. He stood at the bar, big without being tall, maybe half again as broad as the other figures around him, turned even larger by the bulky old mackinaw he wore, his bat-wing chaps the worse for wear. Gotch had just flipped a jigger of whiskey to him, and he took it in a heavy, scarred hand, licking dry lips as he glanced idly around the room. With a distinct effort, Elgera turned toward the faro layout at the other side of the saloon.

"*Señorita* Scorpion." The voice was muffled, coming from the crowd around the bar and tables, and it was taken up, farther away and nearer, and the shift of men was toward this side of the room. A slim Mexican *vaquero* in a fancy *serape* slipped the plush-bottomed chair from beneath the table by the dealer's box, bowing for Elgera to be seated, shoving it in when she was down. She looked up at the ring of sweating faces surrounding the table, turned hazy now and then by rising clouds of tobacco smoke, and she did not try to deny the excitement in her. Even if there was not as much skill in faro as in poker, as Cojo said, the element of chance was still there, and it caught at her.

The drunk *vaquero* on her right was from Durango, and this was the third night straight he had spent at the layout, and he smashed a dirty brown fist down on the enameled cloth. "Take a turn, *señorita,* take a turn. . . ."

Maybe it was the scarred fingers on his shoulder that stopped him. Something like pain was in the grimace he made. He turned part way about, jerking his shoulder to get away, but that was futile. The fingers were indented so deeply his shirt was drawn into a pucker of wrinkles around each one.

"*¿Caramba,*" he gasped abruptly, "*que hace, tu bribón . . . ?*"

Elgera lost the rest of it as he was swung away into the crowd, and the man in the old mackinaw was there, one hand still up in the air where he had let go of the *vaquero*'s shoulder. Elgera stared up at his squinted eyes, and her lips formed his name without sound. *Chisos.* Then she shook her head almost imperceptibly from side to side.

His eyes widened a little as he interpreted her meaning. The men began to shove against him, calling for Elgera to take a turn.

She wanted to smile suddenly, as she saw how little effect their movement had on his square, granitic bulk, and she shuffled the deck and cut and placed it on the dealing box. The men shoved their bets onto the suit of spades enameled in the cloth. High bet was on king and ace.

She waved one hand. "All bets down."

Soda was the exposed, top card of the deck, which did not count, and she slipped it through the slit in the side of the dealer's box, and then slipped the other card of the turn through the slit, placing it face up on the table. The second card was ten of hearts. She raked in the house winnings, and put the two cards of the turn on the case. After the third turn, Elgera saw Bighead towering above all the others, moving through the outer ring of men. He stopped behind Chisos, watching a couple more turns.

"A lot of *hombres* come in just to watch *Señorita* Scorpion," he said finally, "but they do their looking from the bar. If you want to stand this close, *señor,* you'd better do some betting."

Elgera saw the stiffening of Chisos's body. Then he turned, without looking directly at Bighead, and let the crowd close around in front of him. Elgera could see him no more, but she guessed he had gone to buy some chips.

Lupita had begun to sing from somewhere across the room. The rasping huskiness of her voice held a certain sensuous attraction, and she knew how to stir the blood with the swift backbeat of her guitar, but the men about the faro layout paid no attention. Beneath the music, Elgera could hear the shuffle of Lupita's feet as she crossed the floor, dancing as she sang. Elgera dealt the twenty-fifth turn. The last card left in the box was hoc, and did not count. She slipped it out and shuffled the deck again. The drunk *vaquero* from Durango was back again, reeling over the table, plunking a stack of chips on the ace of spades.

"*Señorita* Scorpion." Maybe it was the way he said the name. "*Señorita* Scorpion, you better deal it straight this time. I got my eye on the box this time. Slip one out of the bottom and it'll be the last card you turn."

"Rodriguez," she told him. "I don't think you'd better play any more till you're sober."

"I'll play this table . . ." — he hitched his gun around in front — "I'll play this table drunk or sober, and you can't stop me. Now take a turn . . . take a turn!"

She looked around for Bighead. He was

standing on the edge of the crowd again. She tilted her blonde head toward Rodriguez. Bighead leered, nodding, but did not move inwards. Elgera frowned, tilting her head more sharply than the drunk man. Bighead nodded again, his flushed face still holding that leer, and still did not move. There was a sudden wildness in the way Elgera's tawny brow arched. *All right,* she thought, *all right, don't back me up. Make me handle it? All right. Maybe you think I can't. Maybe you think. . . .*

"Take a turn . . . take a turn."

She jerked soda out of the box, and the next card, slapping them down on the table, and, before the second one was down, Rodriguez let out a wild whoop. *"¡El as . . . el as . . . !"*

"You're looking at soda," Elgera told him. "The turn was the queen."

She started to rake in his chips, but he caught the rake, shouting: "I want you to deal it straight! You pulled that soda off the bottom. It was the last turn. The turn was the ace!"

Elgera threw a last glance at Bighead. He was still standing outside the crowd. Rodriguez jerked the rake off the chips and started to gather them in. Elgera's chair made a sharp scrape as she shoved it back, but she had not risen when that same scarred hand fell on Rodriguez. This time it was on his wrist, instead of his shoulder, and he cried out with the pain.

"*Señorita* Scorpion never took a card from the bottom in her life," said Chisos Owens. "I think you'd better apologize."

"*¡Maldita!*" shouted Rodriguez, and threw his free arm across his body to grab his gun. Chisos let go the man's other wrist and twisted aside slightly to pull his own arm across his body, and, when he came back in, his elbow caught Rodriguez in the belly. The Mexican bent forward with a sick sound and forgot about his gun.

It was only then that Bighead moved in, grabbing Chisos by the arm and spinning him around. "The house will take care of things like that, *señor.*"

"It didn't look like you were doing it," said Chisos.

Elgera was on her feet now, and the crowd had spread away from Chisos and Bighead, hiding this enough so only those at the faro table were aware of what had happened, and the twang of the guitar still came from farther out. Bighead leaned forward slightly, towering above Chisos, and, the way his face was flushed, Elgera knew he had some liquor in him.

"Bighead," she said.

"You better cash in your chips and leave, *señor*," said Bighead.

Elgera saw the way Chisos Owens's shoulders bunched up beneath his heavy mackinaw, and she knew his voice would have a flat sound. "I don't want to."

Rodriguez had recovered from the blow enough to straighten up, his face a sick gray color. "Get the dirty *gringo* out of here, Bighead, or I'll do it for you."

"Are you going to cash in your chips?" said Bighead.

"I haven't used them yet," said Chisos.

"Bighead," cried Elgera, and then: "Chisos, look out . . . !"

Rodriguez had gone for his gun again. Chisos whirled around and grabbed the *vaquero*'s arm just as Rodriguez got his weapon free and hauled it upward, gun and all. The six-shooter exploded toward the ceiling as Chisos levered Rodriguez backward with that arm, throwing him across the table. With the man bent over the layout like that, Chisos raised one huge fist and struck with it as he would with a hammer, hitting Rodriguez full in the face. The table trembled beneath the blow, and Rodriguez slid off without a sound.

"*¡Barrachón,*" roared Bighead, "*gringo*

174

barrachón!" He was on Chisos's back. Chisos whirled beneath the attack, warding off Bighead's first blow with his upflung left arm so that the man's arm went over his shoulder, and Bighead himself crashed into Chisos. Elgera saw Chisos draw back his right fist and swing with the blow. It was as deadly as it was short, and Bighead's air left him with an exploding gasp. Elgera saw Chisos get set to follow it up with one to the face, but then the other men were swarming in.

"*¡Gringos, gringos!*" they were shouting, and whatever happened between Bighead and Chisos after that was lost to Elgera as the mob inundated the two men.

She knew how it would be now, with everyone in it, and she jumped to her chair, yelling — "Texas, Texas!" — and then was on top of the table. "Texas, Texas . . . !"

Still calling, she tried to pick a man who was directly on top of Chisos and kicked him in the head with her spiked-heeled Hyer. He reeled away, clapping his hand to a bloody ear, and she caught another man by the hair, spinning him around till he was faced toward her and then slamming his face down on the table with all her strength. All the resistance of his body collapsed beneath her, and she released his hair to let him slide off the table.

"Texas, Texas . . . !"

Already she could see them answering her shout, two men at first; then three, forming a little knot as they moved across the room; then four, gaining momentum; then five, charging now through the mob of Mexicans between the bar and the faro layout; then seven; and eight, big, wild-eyed six-footers with ten gallon hats instead of sombreros and barrel-leg chaps instead of *chivarras*, plowing a path through the smaller Mexicans like a cut of longhorn Texas steers ramming through a bunch of scrubby Mexican blackhorns.

Chisos was no longer in close to the table. Elgera did not see him, first. She saw the sudden hole appear in the crowd as the men spread back from a wild, slugging, yelling figure in their center, and, when it had grown enough, she could see him fully. Bighead lay on his face at Chisos's feet, and another man sat against the legs of a third, his face twisted, holding a patently broken arm. A pair tried to get Chisos from the back, and he whirled to catch the first one and slung him bodily back against the second, and the both of them crashed into the first ranks of the crowd.

"Come on," bellowed Chisos, "I thought

you were going to throw me out. Come on!"

Another man reeled back into the crowd. He fell into someone, and the men caught the man to keep him from being knocked on backward, and then dropped him aside so he could step into the open. He was no shorter than Chisos, but his slimness made him appear smaller, and his lopsided walk took off some of his actual height.

"Come on," bellowed Chisos, filled with the fighting rage Elgera knew so well, "come on . . . !"

"I'm coming," said the slim man, limping past the Mexican, who sat on the floor holding his broken arm, "I'm coming, *señor*."

"Cojo," cried Elgera, "don't. He'll kill you."

"*¿Qué está?*" shouted one of the men on the outside of the ring. "What is it, *compadres?*"

"El Cojo," said another, and the name passed through the crowd softly, and, as if by tacit agreement, the Texans and the Mexicans stopped fighting at the end of the table, spreading away from the two men on the other side of the layout. Elgera jumped off the table, grabbing a gun from one of the Texan's holsters. She could not see the two men in the center of the crowd now, but, as she fought her way through the press of fetid bodies, she heard Cojo's voice, saying something unintelligible, and Chisos's answer, and then a sudden shuffle of feet. A shout went up from the crowd, drowning the other sounds.

"Cojo," she panted, "Cojo, he'll kill you. . . ."

Then she had broken through, and could see them. It was one of the few times she had ever seen Chisos Owens down. He lay on his back, staring up at the lame man, and there was more surprise on his face than pain. It was not what Elgera had expected, and for that moment she was at a loss. Shaking his head, Chisos got up on one elbow, watching Cojo narrowly. Cojo stood motionless, that faint, ironic smile on his face. Finally Chisos got to his feet, a great square block of a man with his solid legs spread wide beneath his torso and his shoulders thrust forward. He shrugged out of the mackinaw, and his dirty white shirt clung damply with sweat to the roll of muscle that bunched up around his neck like a range bull's. With an abrupt, hoarse sound, he moved in.

"Chisos," said Elgera, and raised the gun halfway, "Cojo." Then she stopped, because she did not know which one it was now, and away down inside her, although she tried to deny it at first, the desire was growing to see just which man would win it if she left it alone.

There was no subterfuge in Chisos. He was waiting for something this time, and he did not rush Cojo, but he moved in steadily without feinting or stalling, and, when he got close enough, he threw his punch. Cojo ducked it, and his feet made a shuffle on the floor. He moved so fast Elgera could not follow it. But it must have been what Chisos was waiting for. He let his first punch go on over Cojo's head without trying to recover it and followed through with his other fist. Both blows must have landed about the same time. Chisos grunted and bent forward with Cojo's fist sinking like a rapier into his unprotected belly. Cojo's head snapped back as Chisos's fist hit him in the face.

It was the quicker man, then. Both of them had been equally staggered, and it was the quicker man. With his body up against Chisos, and both Chisos's arms outflung, Cojo grabbed upward blindly, catching the bigger man by the wrist. Chisos had recovered by then and tried to pull away, and then saw that would be a mistake and tried to strike with his free fist, but he was too late.

Holding Chisos's arm out stiff, Cojo spun him halfway around and kicked both feet out from beneath him with a sideswipe of his leg, and let go the arm to hit Chisos behind the neck as he went down.

Only now could Elgera see how Chisos's blow had taken Cojo. The lame man's face was bleeding down one side, and he passed his hand across his eyes, shaking his head dully. His breath had a torn sound, and he started to say something to Gotch. Then he stopped, because Chisos was getting up again. Once more Elgera had the impulse to try and stop this, and once more than nameless restraint held her back. Chisos rose to his hands and knees.

"*Señor,*" said El Cojo, "don't be a fool. Even an animal knows when to quit. I do not want to kill you." Chisos got to one knee, put his hand on his other knee, drawing a heavy breath. Cojo's voice grew sharper. "*Señor,* I warn you. Don't be a fool. I am past doing it prettily. If you get up again. . . ."

Chisos got up again. He turned with his arms out and went for Cojo that way. Cojo waited for him, and again it was that movement too fast for Elgera to see, drawing a swift, sighing sound from the crowd and Chisos's gasp as Cojo struck. Cojo backed and knocked Chisos's arm down, and struck again. Chisos took it, jerking spasmodically, and kept on going with his other arm out. Cojo knocked that one down and struck once more, crouching in with his shoulder behind the blow, his arm darting in like a blade. Chisos jerked to that one, too, and caught Cojo's arm while it was still in there. Face a set, white mask of pain, Chisos pulled Cojo into him. His blow was with the arm on the other side of his body, so that all Elgera could see was his elbow, bobbing out behind him and then disappearing forward again, but a sick wave of nausea swept her as she heard the dull, fleshy sound it made, and saw Cojo stiffen spasmodically, because she knew what Chisos could do to a man that way.

In that moment, Cojo was rigid against Chisos, and, holding him in there, Chisos drew back his fist to strike again. Then Cojo's weight went backward, and, hanging onto him, Chisos was pulled after. Cojo had enough consciousness left for this, and he hit with his legs jack-knifing up between him and Chisos, and his feet striking Chisos's chest, rolling the heavy man on over his head as they went down. Sucking his breath in with a hoarse gasp, Cojo turned over on his side and got to his feet somehow, and jumped at Chisos while the bigger man was still down.

"I told you," he panted, grabbing Chisos by the hair, "I was through doing it prettily." He lifted Chisos's head and slammed it back against the floor so hard Elgera felt the boards tremble beneath her. Then Cojo straightened, holding his side with one hand, and watched for any sign from Chisos. After a moment, the lame man turned to Gotch. "I guess you can take him out now."

Four 🐎

The moonlight dropped hesitant yellow fingers into the mysterious depths of Santa Helena Cañon, and the rock walls echoed to the incessant roar of the rapids in the Río Grande flowing through the narrow bottom of the gorge. A game trail was the only passage along the northern cliffs, and Elgera moved slowly down its narrow incline, trying to discern movement in the shadows that pooled in the hollows. Finally, the game track met the old Smuggler's Trail which had been used for centuries by Indians and Mexicans, broadening out to a hoof-printed way. Oro Peso lay at the southern end of the gorge, and she was only a mile from the town when the trail dropped onto the sandy beach of the ford. Here she stopped a moment, looking on into the dark chasm, deafened by the ceaseless roar of the rapids farther up. There were some willows drooping near the water, where a man might make his camp, and she moved toward them, parting the first shoots hesitantly.

He had risen and was holding a gun, down

in a hollow that the willows concealed, and his voice was barely audible. "Elgera!"

"I didn't think you were in any condition to travel very far," she said, descending into the gully. "I heard they dropped you at the edge of town."

Patently he was not thinking of that, as he dropped the Bisley back into the holster, moving toward her in an awkward eagerness, opening his mouth to say something, then closing it. He had always been this way, so potent among men, yet so inadequate with women, so inarticulate when it came to expressing his emotions.

"Elgera," he said finally, "when I thought something had happened to you down here. . . ."

"I know, Chisos." She caught his hand. "I know. I felt the same way when Cojo did that to you." She bit her lip, looking at the mess it had made of one side of his face where Cojo had slammed it against the floor. Then she couldn't help the wry little smile. "You know, that's the first time I've ever seen a man whip you."

There was irritation in his voice. "Is that why you didn't stop it?"

"Did you want me to?"

"You know what I'd have done to you if you *had* stopped it." He couldn't help the grin, then he sobered. "That isn't the point. You were calling to both of us. Do I figure that wrong?"

She turned away from him, knowing what he meant as she asked: "What do you mean?"

"Cojo is good-looking . . . in his way."

Elgera met his eyes again. "Chisos, it isn't that."

"Isn't it?" he asked. "Why have you staked your horse in his pasture, then?"

"Something's going on down here," she said.

"That's what I'm saying."

She stamped her foot. "I don't mean that. Why do you keep twisting what I say?"

"Maybe it's already twisted."

She was driven to it. "All right, so maybe I like Cojo. Is that what you want to hear? Maybe he's been nice to me, or interesting, or fascinating. Maybe I've never met anybody quite like him. Maybe that's why I didn't try to stop the fight. Maybe I wanted to see how he matched you."

Chisos was suddenly contrite, holding out his hand that way again. "Elgera. . . ."

"No!" She was kept going by her anger now. "You threw this dally. I don't blame you for being jealous. Cojo's a handsome man. Any woman would find him interesting. Maybe he *is* the reason I'm staying down here."

"Elgera, don't be like this." He was flushing. "It's not that. I didn't mean to say it that way. I've just been so knotted up inside, thinking maybe you were . . . were. . . ."

"All right," she said sullenly. "Let's drop it. There *is* something beside Cojo keeping me here. I was trying to tell you that."

"The cattle?" he asked hopefully. "That's how I found you were missing. I dropped over to your outfit about the time your brother got back from chousing after those rustled cattle and found out you hadn't come in. I took right out after you."

"Natividad and I followed about fifty head of our Circulo S cattle as far as Rustler's Crossing," she said. "Then we lost the trail and got separated trying to find it again south of the Río. My brother must have figured I'd gone back to the Santiago. We'd agreed on that if we got separated. But I'd found the trail again and staked my horse, when I thought I was nearing the rustled cattle. I missed on that, and, when I got back to where my horse had been, she was gone. It took me most of the day to reach Oro Peso."

"Got any leads?"

She shook her head. "It isn't the cattle,

186

now. That trail's too cold. You know I couldn't get anything out of the Mexicans if they knew I was after my Circulo S steers. Staying around the Río wouldn't do any good. It's not that. I told you . . . something's going on down here."

"Penasco?"

Maybe it was the way he said it that brought her head up sharply. "What do you know?"

"I saw a dead man marked with his *rúbrica*. Is that why you didn't want to know me at Cojo's?"

She shrugged. "I thought it would be better if they didn't know our connection. Cojo trusts me, I think, to a certain extent."

"He's mixed up in it?"

She studied her feet, shuffling them in the sand. "I don't know."

"Or don't want to know?"

Her eyes flashed. "Chisos, don't start that again. If Cojo's mixed up in it. . . ."

The willows sighed behind her, and she was already whirling toward them as Chisos went for his Bisley. But he had never been a flash with a gun, and it would not have mattered much anyway, since the man standing above them on the bank of the gully already had his gold-chased Remington in his hand. Elgera's voice sounded

187

muffled, even to her, against the roar of the river.

"Bighead," she said.

It was south of the Río Grande about half a mile, in a copse of cottonwoods sheltered by a low red ridge. Másomenos got up from the fire with some effort as the three of them came through the trees, coughing a little in the dust raised by the nervous cattle milling around on the alkali flats past the grove.

"Put on some *café*, Másomenos," said Bighead mockingly. "Can't you see we have visitors?"

Másomenos clapped a fat hand to his head, rocking backward. "*Ai, caramba,* I knew it . . . I knew it. I told you we would have trouble if you didn't quit looking around for *Señorita* Scorpion, Bighead."

"They were following us," said Bighead. "I found them at Rustler's Crossing." He saw how Elgera kept looking out toward the cattle, and laughed. "Is that what you were looking for, *señorita?* They are not your cattle. They are ours."

"*Más o menos,*" said the fat man.

"*Sí,*" grinned Bighead. "More or less. At least they are more ours than they are the man's who used to own them, and less his now than they were at one time."

"I thought you worked for Cojo," said Elgera.

"Many people make that mistake," said Bighead, and he was watching Chisos, and he was no longer grinning. "I think I owe you something, *Señor* . . . ah . . . *Señor* . . . ?"

"*Señor* Chisos Owens," supplied the man standing outside the firelight, and then he moved in so they could see him.

"Tequila!" said Chisos.

Elgera saw the strange pocks marking his face, and her first thought was Lupita, and then she saw the deep, gruesome gash through the bridge of his arrogant nose, and she remembered it, and looked at his hands. He caught the glance, and a sardonic amusement was in his smile.

"*Sí, señorita,* the manacles are gone now." He looked toward Chisos. "It is unfortunate I could not be there to identify you in Oro Peso, but I was . . . ah . . . attending to other matters, eh? I understand you weren't recognized. They just carried you out of town and dumped you like they would any *barrachón* who had crossed El Cojo. Perhaps things would have come out differently if you had been known. Perhaps what we have to do now would have been taken care of."

"*¿Compadres,*" said Másomenos uncomfortably, "is it absolutely *necesario?* Maybe if

189

we just ask them to go home? After all, they didn't actually see whose cattle. . . ."

"*Punto en boca*," snarled Bighead. "Stick it in your ass, and tie this Chisos up. I owe him something for this evening."

"Don't be foolish," said Tequila. "There's no use doing anything before. . . ."

"Before what?" Elgera broke in.

Tequila inclined his head toward her. "I thought you understood, *señorita*."

Suddenly she did understand fully, for the first time. He saw it in her face, and smiled faintly. She waved her hand at the milling cattle out on the flats.

"Just for a bunch of cattle?"

"No, not just for a bunch of cattle," said Bighead. "Our necks enter into it. You did not stay down here because you liked the scenery."

"Cojo made me a proposition," she said hotly.

Bighead grinned evilly. "I'm not surprised. And it fitted in nicely with your plans, no? Did you think you could find out who got your cattle wet by sticking around the Río?"

"I found out, didn't I?"

"And now you think you'll go back and identify us?" said Bighead. "I have been in the business a long time, *señorita*, and I still

190

wear a nice soft collar around my neck. Nobody's going to put a rope there."

Chisos must have understood now, too, because he bent forward, his voice intense. "But she's a woman."

"Some of the Mexicans don't think so," grinned Tequila. "They think she's a wildcat. Or a scorpion?"

"Don't be a fool. You can't do that. Not to a woman. Not just over a bunch of cattle like this . . . to a woman."

"It is like Bighead says," murmured Tequila. "There are a number of parties . . . quite a number . . . who would like to exchange our nice soft collars for a rope, if they had something definite on which to act. It was due to somebody's loose mouth that I fell into *Capitán* Zaragosa's hands the other night, and I would be kicking my heels ten feet above the Plaza Militar in Mexico City right now if fortune had not favored me. I don't want it to happen again."

Chisos's eyes had grown narrow as the man spoke. "Or maybe it isn't for just a bunch of cattle."

"*¿Qué está?*" asked Tequila.

"Real Penasco," said Chisos.

A hush dropped after his word, and the sudden snapping of the fire caused Másomenos to jump. "*Dios,*" he said. "Don't

191

say it like that. What about Penasco?"

"You know what about Penasco," Chisos told him.

"*Más o menos,*" said the fat man, "more or less."

"Másomenos means what about Penasco . . . specifically?" said Tequila, his eyes glittering with a new interest.

"Specifically," said Chisos, "you did a nice job on *Capitán* Zaragosa the other night, Real."

"What about Zaragosa . . . ?" Tequila started to say, and then checked himself. He stood there a moment, staring at Chisos. "Oh," he said finally, almost inaudibly. "Oh."

"What job on Zaragosa?" asked Bighead angrily. "What are you talking about?"

Chisos looked at Tequila's hairy hand. "You know what he's talking about. Ask him where his ring is."

Tequila threw back his head to laugh. "A big man, *señores,* with shoulders like the *toros* they used to breed for the bullrings, and he is never without his short blue *capuz,* and he was in the smallpox epidemic at Hermosillo in 'Sixty-Seven."

"Tequila," shouted Bighead. "What are you talking about?"

"*Nada, compadre, nada,*" said Tequila, his

laughter stopping. "A little joke between *Señor* Chisos and I, that's all. We have had the pleasure of meeting before, you see. He was telling me of what happened after we parted."

Bighead's eyes widened. "You mean Zaragosa . . . ?"

"Has been honored with the *Rúbrica de Penasco*," said Tequila, and he looked at Bighead, and something passed between them. Másomenos put a fat hand over his mouth, staring wide-eyed at them. Finally Bighead jerked his Remington at Chisos.

"I told you to tie him up, Másomenos," he growled.

"And I told you there wasn't any use tying him up," said Tequila.

"No man does that to me," said Bighead. "Tie him up, Másomenos. I'm going to give him a pistol-whipping he'll remember when he reaches hell."

"Cojo said he never saw anybody else whip you," said Elgera.

She saw Chisos's big frame draw taut for a moment, and then he must have understood her intent, for he took the cue. "Yeah," he said. "And now you have to tie me up."

"Cojo was right," said Bighead. "Nobody ever whipped me. And I don't have to tie you up. I'll. . . ."

"Bighead," said Tequila. "You won't do anything. You won't do anything but get rid of them right here and right now."

"And from Mexico City to the Red River they'll be able to say Chisos Owens whipped Bighead," said Elgera.

"Nobody will ever say that," growled Bighead, and tossed his gun to Másomenos and moved toward Chisos. "And I don't have to tie you up, either."

"No!" Tequila's voice turned Bighead toward him. The pockmarked man had drawn his Colt, and it was pointed at Bighead.

Elgera saw Chisos take a breath and was moving herself even as he jumped for Bighead. She caught Másomenos by the arm and spun him around, throwing him off balance as Chisos threw himself at Bighead, caught the huge Quill about the waist, and heaved him at Tequila. Tequila tried to jump backward and fire at Chisos all at once, but Bighead was in between them, hurtling toward Tequila, and the bullet went wide. Then the Quill hit Tequila, and they both staggered a few steps across the ground, trying to keep from falling, and then went down together. Elgera grasped Bighead's Remington in Másomenos's fat hand, trying to twist it free.

"No, *señorita*, no," squealed the fat man,

throwing his bulk backward. She was still hanging onto the Remington and was pulled off her feet, falling against Másomenos. Then he grunted above her, with the thud of a weight crashing into him, and she cried out with his gross body coming down on top of her. Breath knocked from her, she heard Másomenos cry out from a blow, and his hand relaxed around the gun butt. She managed to squeeze from beneath him with the Remington in her hand. Chisos Owens was straddling Másomenos, his great fist brought back for another blow. Tequila had rolled from beneath Bighead and was sprawled on his belly with his Colt across one forearm. Holding the Remington in both hands, Elgera fired. She saw the slug kick dirt into Tequila's face, and he reared up to his knees, swearing bitterly as he pawed the acrid alkali from his eyes. From the herd, riders were coming, and Bighead rolled toward the saddles piled beyond the fire where Elgera caught several saddle boots sticking out from under the mound of gear.

"Chisos," she cried, snapping a shot at Bighead and then shifting the gun to one hand so she could grab Chisos Owens. He came off Másomenos with his head jerking from side to side, and she knew he was looking for a gun. Bighead had reached the gear, snaking a Winchester from one of the boots, and the riders coming in began firing, and Elgera shoved Chisos toward the cottonwoods climbing the ridge. He was a stubborn man, but he must have realized the futility of trying to stay and fight all of them, and he crashed into the timber alongside of her as Bighead began levering the .30-30. The bullets made a whining rattle through the foliage, and beneath the bang of the gun Tequila was shouting something. Then, abruptly, the noise behind them ceased. It was Chisos who halted Elgera, his fingers digging painfully into her arm. Behind them they could hear a faint movement, then silence again.

"Little slower now," muttered Chisos.

It was painful, moving that slow, but they made little sound. After a while a hooty owl began calling from higher up. They reached the ridge top and looked for the fire on the Santa Helena flats below and behind them, and could not see it. A shroud of night covered the land.

"Must have doused it," growled the big man, crouching beside her. "They'll expect us to head for Santa Helena Cañon. Let's take the opposite direction a piece."

They moved southward along the

shoulder of the ridge so as not to be skylighted. Whenever they stopped to listen, he stood close enough for the heat of his body to warm her, and she caught the vagrant smell of tobacco and sage and sweaty leather emanating from him and liked the familiarity of it, somehow. Finally he sensed her looking up at his face, and turned. She touched his arm.

"Chisos. . . ."

Whatever else she would have said was stopped by the silhouette on the ridge top. It appeared from nowhere, apparently, without discernible sound, standing motionless. Chisos turned back, following the direction of her glance, and even in the semidarkness she saw the blood leave his sun-darkened face, turning the cheeks an odd, putty color.

"El Morzillo," he almost whispered, "Penasco." Then, with a low, muffled sound in his throat, he scrambled upward. Elgera's thumb caught at the big single-action hammer on the Remington as she jumped after him. The rider was silhouetted for another instant up there, a black man on a black horse, his short cloak whipping in the breeze. Then he was gone, and it was Chisos Owens's bulk surging up against the sky. Mesquite ripped at Elgera's *charro* leggings as she stumbled up behind him, seeing Chisos's silhouette drop behind the somber bulk of the ridge. She reached the top panting heavily, hesitating a moment before skylighting herself. The shot came as she crossed the crest, and she dropped into a pocket on the other side, the adobe hard against her stomach. Lying there with the cocked Remington held in both hands, she tried to hear any other sound. It was an old Comanche trick, holding the mouth open to improve the hearing, but it did no good.

"Chisos," she sobbed, and began stumbling down the slope in a crouch, rattling through mesquite and stabbing herself on the hidden malignancy of horsemainer, desperately seeking something tangible to battle, the moonlight catching the spasmodic jerk of her blonde head from one side to the other as she sought him. She was halfway down the slope before she came across Chisos. A suffocation filled her as she knelt beside his big frame, sprawled out in a clump of brush. He lay on his back with his right cheek turned upward. She put her hand flat on his chest. It was still warm, but there was no movement of breathing. And all the while she was staring at his cheek. The warm, thick blood from the bullet hole in his chest seeped through her fingers, and still she crouched there, motionless, looking at his cheek. Finally she took a heavy, broken breath, and her eyes moved away from Chisos's face until they were turned blankly toward the sky. She was crying softly, and the tears were salty in her mouth, and the lump in her throat and breast was something that would be there always.

"Penasco," she said, and it was hardly audible, "you think you've sworn vengeance . . . then hear mine. I won't rest . . . I won't stop . . . I won't die . . . until I've found you."

◣◢ Five

The whole thing was unfortunate. Standing there at the bar, he couldn't help thinking that, over and over. The whole thing. If only she had not come. He twirled the jigger of expensive bourbon idly in his long, supple fingers, studying the amber liquid. There had been enough other women. He squinted his eyes, trying to remember the first one. María? *Sí*, María, with hair like midnight across the Sierras and eyes like the banked coals of a fire, and he had told her so, and that had been that. Quartil? Had she been next? Or Barranca, in Durango? It did not matter much. It did not matter whether they were black-haired or red, or black-eyed or blue, they had been with him a while, or he had been with them, and he had enjoyed them, or they had enjoyed him, and that was about all that mattered, and he had considered none of it unfortunate, because, when the time came to part, it had always been easy enough. He set the glass down with an abrupt thud. Why, then, should this be different? There had been blondes before. There had been blondes with eyes like this, and a mouth like this, and a figure like this. Then he was looking at himself in the mirror, unable to stop the wry smile on his lips. *But not quite like this, eh?* The smile turned to a small laugh. *No, not quite like this, not ever quite like this.*

He knew the vagrant wish that he had met her sooner. Perhaps things could have been different. Five years ago, or six. Then he closed his hand angrily around the drink, tossing it off. *Things could never have been different.*

"Cojo." The call turned him, and he saw Lupita standing in the short hallway, still wearing her black velvet basque beneath a short leather riding jacket, her skirt replaced by a split riding habit. He limped along the bar toward her and inclined his head toward his office door behind where she stood. Shutting the heavy portal after they were inside the room, he glanced at the alkali on her boots.

"I was down at Uncle Parco's," she said nervously, turning to study his face. Then she came closer. "Cojo, you've got to help me with Tequila."

"He's in trouble again?"

"No, no," she said softly, not meeting his eyes. "But if you could only keep him here for a few days. . . . Get that blonde out of my room and he could stay there."

"You mean hide him?" said Cojo. He turned to the desk, taking a cheroot from the box, trying to hide the anger in him. "I told you I was through when I had Gotch file those manacles off Tequila. I'm getting tired of your cattle-rustling brother, Lupita. Bighead causes me enough trouble with his constant drinking. I told you it was the last time I would help Tequila. If he's in trouble again, it's his own fault."

"He isn't in trouble, Cojo," she said desperately. "I swear it. I only want you to keep him here so he *won't* get into trouble. I'll promise you he won't cause you any difficulty, Cojo."

He bit off the end of the cheroot, noticing the slight tremor already in his hand. *Damn this girl.* He looked at her pockmarked face. What had he ever seen in her? A certain sensuous attraction, he had told himself, that other men missed because they only saw the scars? It almost made him laugh now. *Damn her!*

"You were down at your Uncle Parco's," he said, looking at the alkali on her boots again. "I didn't think you had to cross Santa Helena flats to reach his *jacal*."

"I took the long way 'round." She came

closer, trying to catch his hand. "Please, Cojo. . . ."

"You're lying," he said softly, controlling the growing anger in him with an effort. "You were with your brother. Tequila's been running wet cattle down the Smuggler's Trail again, and you've been with him."

"No, no." She threw herself on him, twining her arms around his neck. "Please, Cojo . . . for me . . . take Tequila in here for a few days. You'll do it for me . . . ?"

"Let go," he hissed, jerking his mouth off her wet lips, getting his arm between their bodies and twisting around as he levered her away, thrusting her back so hard she stumbled across the room and brought up against a wall. She stood there with her palms flat against the adobe, small breasts heaving, her eyes smoldering at him.

"You used to like my kisses," she panted.

"Get out." There was a terrible restraint to the shaking intensity of his voice.

"It's that woman," she said, almost inaudibly. "*Señorita* Scorpion."

"Get out." His whole body was trembling now, and the rage was turning that strange glow in his eyes to a burning flame.

"I'm right, then." Her voice was louder now. "It *is* that woman."

"Get out," he said and could hardly hear

it himself, and it was the last time he would say it.

"Do you think you can get rid of me that easy? Just because of a little blonde . . . ?"

Her words cut off in a scream as he leaped toward her, catching her with one hand about the neck, flinging her toward the door. She spun around once before she struck the portal, flailing with her arms to try and keep her balance, and the door shuddered with her weight going into it, and she slid helplessly down it onto the floor.

"I told you," he shouted, standing over her, his eyes blazing, his whole body shaking violently. "I told you . . . I told you."

She stared up at him, sobbing brokenly. There was pain in her face, but, more, there was fear, for it was the first time he had revealed this side of himself to her. She tried to speak, and choked on her words. She got to her knees, and then rose against the door, hands clawing the carved panels for support, staring, fascinated, into his burning eyes. Finally she got the words out.

"Yes, I'll go, but not before I tell you. Your blonde sweetheart ran out on you last night. The *hombre* you beat up is Chisos Owens. He's *her* man. Why do you think he was here in the first place? She's gone to him now, and you'll never see her again."

With a broken, animal sound, he caught her, both hands on her neck this time. "No!" he shouted, that rage sweeping all sane thought from his head, "you're lying . . . you're lying . . . you're lying . . . !"

With her head thrown back, she clawed at his hands, her face twisting from side to side, the words blurting out in a strangled sob. "You can see easy . . . enough. You can see. Look in . . . her room. See . . . if I'm lying. See . . . see. . . ."

He stood there a moment longer, holding her like that. Then he released her, his breath making a harsh, terrible sound. She clutched at her neck, gasping for air, crying with the agony. He opened the door and crossed the hall, hearing her rise and follow him, coughing and crying. Run out on him? He flung the bedroom door open. That was what he got for letting himself dream of a blonde with eyes that flashed like. . . .

"What is it, Cojo?"

Elgera raised her head off the pillow, blinking sleepily, her hair tumbling in a shimmering, tousled cascade about her pink, flushed face, and for that moment the beauty of her held him speechless.

"What is it?" she repeated, putting a white arm out over the cover.

"Nothing," he spoke through thin lips.

"Just get dressed. I want to see you."

He turned around to find Lupita standing pale and wide-eyed in the doorway to his office, staring past him into the bedroom. "But I thought . . . ," she muttered. "Tequila told me. . . ."

"Tequila told you?" he scoffed. "Tequila told you what? Is this the way you were planning to get rid of Elgera?" He drew in a heavy breath, his rage under control now, lacerating himself for having let her see it. "I'm not going to ask you again, Lupita. Get out."

She stared a moment, mouth open, then, with a wild little cry, flung herself to her knees, clutching him about the knees. "No, Cojo, don't," she sobbed hopelessly, "please, Cojo, I'll do anything for you, be anything . . . your slave, Cojo . . . your slave . . . anything . . . *Madre de Dios,* please, please, for God's sake . . . !"

He stood rigidly, filled with disgust, letting her go on until she realized how utterly silent he was. Finally she trailed off, staring up at the implacable will in his face. She must have understood the futility of any more display. Her leather skirt rustled dimly as she drew away from him, and her face was dead white.

"I guess I knew it would be this way . . . from the first. I guess I knew what you were.

I couldn't help it. All bad, Cojo. You never had a friend in your life . . . man or woman. You never loved a woman in your life, me or Elgera or any other woman." There was something terrible about her dry whisper, as she backed down the hall. "You're all bad, and I knew it from the first, and I couldn't help it . . . I can't help it now, and you're not through with me yet. If I can't have you, no other woman can. You're not through with me yet!"

One of Cojo's *criados* had cleaned Elgera's *charro* suit, and the roses sewn down the seam of the trouser leg appeared a bright red in the light as she stepped into Cojo's office. He took the last pull on the cheroot and ground its butt into a hammered silver ashtray on the *escritorio*.

"What was all that in the hall?" she said.

He shrugged, studying her eyes, seeing the faint redness of the lids. "Lupita was having one of her spells. She gets them every time I look at another woman."

"Oh?" She tilted her head to one side, smiling quizzically.

He looked at her a long moment, drawing his lips in. He would have done this for no other woman, he realized. For a moment he was filled with a poignancy he had never known. Just standing there, looking at her. Perhaps it was foolish; perhaps what Lupita had claimed were not all lies. It did not matter now, but it would matter later. He knew that. That was why it had to be done now — while he was filled with it and blind to anything else.

"Something out in the corral for you," he said.

The corrals behind the Cueva de Cojo were more extensive than those usually found backing one of these border structures. There were several covered sheds housing a row of stalls. The horse in the stall at the end stood in deep shadow, and Elgera apparently did not see its true color till they were almost there. Then Cojo saw the surprised widening of her eyes, and the smile breaking over her face, and he felt pain at her pleasure, for it meant that she was happy at being free to leave.

"La Rubia," she cried, and the palomino in the shed suddenly tried to back out of her headstall, kicking and squealing excitedly.

"One of my men picked it up a couple of days ago south on the Río," said Cojo as the girl moved in and unhitched the animal. "She had been grazing free, I guess, since you lost her."

Elgera had the palomino backed out now, running fingers through her silky blonde mane to clear out the burrs and thorns matted there, and she frowned across the mare's back at Cojo. "A couple of days ago?"

He moved up against the horse so he would be that close to Elgera, meeting the girl's blue eyes across the mare's withers. "I know that wasn't very fair, Elgera, but I couldn't help it. That's the way I feel. I knew you would leave the minute you got your horse. It's been here two days now, but I couldn't help it." He stopped, that confusion in him again, because he had never told a woman this before in sincerity. He had told them enough times before, because that's the kind he was, but he had never meant it really, and now that he did mean it, for the first time, he could not find the words. He took a breath, running his hand across the horse's golden coat, and then let the breath out in a frustrated way, unwilling to meet her eyes, and then took another breath, and spoke. "I thought maybe you felt the same way. Sometimes when you looked at me . . . if I hadn't thought that, I would have told you when we first found the horse. But there *were* times." He raised his glance helplessly to her. "I mean. . . ."

Her hand was warm on his across the horse's back. "I think I know what you mean, Cojo."

For that moment, meeting her eyes, he felt an exaltation. Whatever he had done or been before had no significance, and whatever he might do again. Only this moment. He stepped back from the horse, one of his rare smiles lighting his face.

"Maybe you'd like to try her out, after so many days," he said. "The saddle's in the stall."

He did not make the mistake of helping Elgera put on the rig, knowing the insult that would have held. She heaved the big, hand-stamped Porter down off the bars and slung it on the palomino with a casual skill, cinching up the latigos in swift tugs. By that time, Cojo had gotten a sorrel from one of the open corrals and put a Mexican-tree kack on it. He saw the joy in her as Elgera swung aboard the palomino, reining the mare out of the corrals.

Cojo headed them down an alley that led between the outlying hovels of Oro Peso and into the foothills north of town. Riding beside Elgera with the wind fluttering her long blonde hair, Cojo thought the spring had never smelled so sweet. The scent of whitebrush in a draw came up to him like honey on the breeze, and every hoofbeat kicked up rich brown earth beneath them, and a pair of Sonora deer flushed from a gully and bounded across in front of them and made the girl laugh. This was the way it felt, then. This was the way it affected a man. For forty years he had thought he'd been living, and he had not lived at all. And now it had come to him. . . .

He stopped her on the crest of the foot-hills, watching the rise and fall of her breasts beneath the silk shirt as she breathed heavily from the hard ride, raising his eyes to her face as the deck of cards appeared in his hands. "Cut you?"

She looked surprised. "This is becoming a bad habit. Anyway, they aren't fair odds. Once would give me an even break. If you keep it up like this, you're bound to win, sooner or later. I'd be playing against my-self."

"Don't you understand?" he said. "This is the last time."

Something darkened her eyes. "What do you mean?"

"Cut!" he demanded.

Still watching him, she cut the deck in his palm, then drew a card at his nod. He took one, and they turned them face up. She had a ten of clubs to his three of diamonds.

"*Suerte,*" he shrugged, "fate." He put the cards back into his pocket. "I was sort of hoping it would be my high card this time. I would really have liked a kiss before we said *adiós!*"

"*¿Adiós?*" The understanding was in her face now. "But you said . . . you said . . . ?"

"What did I say?"

"The way you felt," she muttered, staring at him. "You told me you didn't let me know when you first found the horse because of the way you felt."

He nodded. "*Sí.*"

"Then why now," she said, a heat entering her voice. "If you didn't want me to leave then, why do you want me to go now? You said you thought maybe I felt the same way. Maybe I do, Cojo. Maybe I don't want to go."

He pulled his sorrel over against her palomino, the softness of her leg pressing into his. He tried to find any guile in her eyes, and there was none. For a moment, the weakness swept him like a flood, and all his resolve was gone.

"Maybe you feel the same way?" he said almost inaudibly.

Her voice was hardly louder. "I've never known anyone like you, Cojo. Only cowhands and ranchers and farmers. When they put their hands on a woman, it's like they were bulldogging a steer. It's different . . . when *you* touch a woman." She stopped a moment, and up close like this he could see the little lines of strain about her mouth. It did not detract from her beauty, but it caused him a moment's wonder. Then she brought her face closer, almost whispering it. "You wouldn't have to cut me for that kiss now, and it wouldn't necessarily have to be *adiós*."

He had never wanted anything so much in his life, but he pulled his horse away abruptly, forcing his voice to be hard. "No. The Chisos Mountains are just ahead. Past them is your Santiago. Your saddlebags contain enough tortillas and cured *carne* to see you through."

She stiffened in her saddle, and he realized she was staring past him down the road. He heard the horses coming then, and his Mexican-tree rig creaked with his turning. They had ridden hard, Tequila and Bighead, and they drew their lathered animals to a halt with vicious tugs on the cruel spade bits.

"Where did you find her?" asked Bighead thickly. He leaned forward in his saddle, his short leather jacket flapping away to reveal the scars of the musculature of his chest.

"You got back to Oro Peso pretty quick, *señorita*. I guess you didn't get much sleep."

Cojo glanced involuntarily at the girl's eyes, and then the alkali on Bighead's wooden-heeled Mexican boots caught his glance.

Bighead reeled back in the saddle, sensuous mouth twisting defiantly. "Sure I was down at Santa Helena flats. To hell with you. We ran a bunch of Big Box steers from north of the rim. I told you I wasn't going to stop handling cattle just because you wanted me to, Cojo. I been running *ganados* across the Río since I was ten years old, and no lame *hombre* is going to keep me from making a living. And no blonde *señorita*, either. She was down at the flats last night with that Chisos Owens, and she saw the cattle we were running. I'm not letting her go back to the Big Box and tell them who borrowed a few of their *ganados*."

"Lupita saw you?" asked Cojo.

"This morning," growled Bighead. "She was coming from her Uncle Parco's."

"And you told her about Elgera?"

"Tequila did," said Bighead. "Now let's have the blonde."

"Nobody is taking Elgera anywhere," said Cojo. "She's going home."

"The hell!" shouted Bighead, spurring his

horse to try and get around Cojo. "We're taking her."

"No," said Cojo, putting a boot into the sorrel's kidney that made it jump between Bighead and the girl. "Ride, Elgera!"

"No, Cojo, I can't. . . ."

"I'm giving you this chance. Ride, I tell you, ride . . . !" Then he saw Bighead's shoulder rise, and kicked his feet out of the stirrups so he would be freed completely, and jumped. All the rest was a confused action to him, his attention focused on Bighead's thick arm as he grabbed it the instant his body struck the man, both of them going on over Bighead's horse. Bighead's Remington exploded, but it was pointing downward due to Cojo's grip on his arm. Then they struck the ground with Bighead beneath, and Cojo tried to pull Bighead's gun from his hand as he rolled free. He sensed the movement behind him, and took it for the horses, and then heard the creak of saddle leather, and the girl's cry, and knew the movement was more than the animals, and then the blow on his head blotted out any perception, and there was no movement about him any more, or sound, or anything.

⁺⁺⁺ Six

There were vague mutterings somewhere above Chisos Owens, and the scent of wood-smoke in his nostrils, and a heavy pain beating in his chest. *If I'm dead,* he thought, *this sure is hell, because it hurts that much.* Then he opened his eyes and saw the *viga* poles above him and knew it wasn't hell because they wouldn't build their houses out of adobe down there. He tried to sit up, but something was holding him down — or somebody.

"*Señor* Chisos?" asked the woman. She had her hand against his head.

"Yeah," he said. "What's left of me."

"You were shot in the chest," she said. "Parco said it was not a lung, or you would be coughing blood."

"The blonde *señorita* left you here," said an old man's voice, and Chisos guessed that must be Parco. "She thought you were dead. She was filled with grief, but there seemed to be some reason she could not wait and see us bury you. It was after she left we found you were not *muerto*. No, *señor*, you must not move . . . !"

But Chisos had already sat up on the *felpudo* of straw and blankets, shaking his head groggily. The woman on her knees beside him had a pockmarked face, and there was a strange, driven light in her eyes as she stared at him. He had seen her before.

"You dance at the Cueva de Cojo?" he asked.

"*Sí,*" she agreed. "I am Lupita. I was there the night Cojo whipped you. Parco here is my *tío* . . . my uncle." Her small bosom began to rise and fall more swiftly, and that strange light grew brighter in her eyes. "*Señorita* Scorpion is your *querida?*"

"Not exactly," he grunted, passing his hand tentatively across his throbbing chest, feeling the thick softness of cotton bandage there. "She knows well enough how I feel about her, but she's never said right out how she feels about me. Sometimes I think she does, and sometimes. . . ."

"It doesn't matter what she feels," said Lupita swiftly, almost angrily. "If you love her, you aren't going to sit here and let her get killed."

The stiffening of his body brought fresh pain. "Killed?"

"*¡Sí, sí!*" said Lupita, grabbing him by the shoulder, "she is trying to find Real Penasco, isn't she? That's what she stayed here for. She came down because of some cattle, but she stayed to find Real Penasco."

"No," he said, "no. . . ."

"Never mind," Lupita dismissed him. "Don't try to deny it. I know." Something savage entered her voice. "Would you like to know who Real Penasco is?"

"I already know," he said.

"Do you? Then you'd better reach him before he kills Elgera Douglas."

Chisos tried to get up, but the old man caught at him. "Lupita, why are you inciting him like this? He cannot be moved."

"Leggo," muttered Chisos hazily. "What about Penasco?" He grabbed the girl abruptly, his big hands drawing a cry of pain from her. "If you know where Penasco is, you'd better tell me. . . ."

"I will, I will," she gasped, and he got the idea it was not him making her do it. "There is an old cave in the walls of Santa Helena Cañon. There are a lot of caves there. The Indians say it was once the home of a vanished race who used the *atl-atl* instead of bows and arrows. . . ."

"I don't care about that," he almost shouted. "What about Elgera?"

"*Señor*, let her go, please," quavered the old man. "Lupita, what are you doing? You don't know anything of Penasco."

"But I do, I do," panted Lupita.

"Tell me," roared Chisos, shaking her.

"In this cave, Penasco keeps his horse, El Morzillo, named after the black war horse of Cortés. Whenever he has found another of the men who betrayed him, he goes to the cave for his horse and cape and ring."

"What good does that do?" he asked bitterly, his breathing hoarse with the pain in him. "I just go there and wait till he comes? The hell...."

"No, no" — she was almost incoherent now — "he'll be there. You've got to hurry."

"How do you know he'll be there?"

"He will. I tell you ... he will. If you don't stop him, Elgera will be killed!"

"Let her go." The old man was still pawing at Chisos. "Let her go."

Chisos released Lupita and turned on him. "Have you got a horse?"

"Somewhat of a horse," said Parco weakly. "But it is all I possess."

"Take mine," Lupita told him in a last passionate burst, "out front."

As he stumbled out the door, Lupita collapsed onto the floor, sobbing hopelessly and dully. Chisos Owens wondered what had driven her to this. Her horse was a wiry little claybank with half a dozen brands scarring its body, some of them blotted out, one noticeably altered. He had trouble mounting, and, when he finally got his big frame into the saddle, he leaned over the slick horn and retched with the agony. *They really put one through me,* he thought, *giddap little horse* — and booted its kidneys — *they really put one through me.*

The claybank had a hard gallop that was sheer hell all the way to the Río Grande. Chisos passed Santa Helena flats and the ridge they had climbed the night before and realized Parco's hovel must be visible from the ridge for Elgera to have taken him there. He forded the river to the old trail extending down the wall of Santa Helena Cañon, the gorge filled with the deafening thunder of the rapids. The trail rose from the sandy shelf constituting the bank, passing the first caves crumbling in the side of the escarpment. A foam rose from below, damp and chill and somehow forbidding.

He was halfway up the side of the frowning cliff when he rounded an eroded formation and saw the movement from one of the potholes that passed for a cave ahead. The roaring river below covered whatever sound his horse made, so he did not dismount. They had left his Bisley in its holster, and he got the big gun out as he urged the claybank up the trail. The trail broadened into a small, grassed-over plateau, and Chisos had reached the near edge of this when the man in the blue *capuz* came fully from the cave across the plateau, leading a black stallion. He must have seen Chisos before he had his right foot in the stirrup. Since the night Zaragosa had been killed, Chisos had retained an idea of Penasco's true identity, and this came as a distinct shock that robbed him of all reaction.

"El Cojo!" he said.

Her hands were sweating on the reins. The breeze was sweeping up off the river, but nonetheless her hands were sweating on the reins. Elgera sat, stiff and pale, on La Rubia, riding between Bighead and Tequila. When Elgera had seen Tequila strike Cojo from behind and had realized it was the only thing that would divert them from killing him, she had spurred her horse past Bighead, racing down the road toward town. Where the road crossed the old Smuggler's Trail, she had met Másomenos. He was forking a scrawny mule and must have fallen behind Bighead and Tequila, and he drove the mule head-on into Elgera, unhorsing them both. By the time she had collected her wits, Bighead and Tequila drew their blowing animals to a halt above her, and that was all. Now they were trotting down the Smuggler's Trail toward the gorge of the river.

"I don't see how you missed Cojo," Bighead was saying. "I thought you hit him harder than that."

Bighead had held Elgera at the fork in the road while Tequila and Másomenos had gone back for Cojo, and Tequila's anger now was plain in his pockmarked face. "I hit him pretty hard," he said acridly.

"He was gone when we got there," said Másomenos. "We found his sorrel halfway down the road from us, but he was gone when we got there."

"Oh, shut up," said Tequila.

"At least, let's get rid of this girl before she causes us any more trouble," snarled Bighead.

"Why did *El Dios* give you such a big *cabeza,* if he did not mean to put any brains in it?" wondered Tequila. "Kill the girl right on the road and leave her lying here, I suppose?"

"We could dump her in the river," suggested Bighead.

"And have maybe a hundred *peones* see us carrying her dead body from here to the river?" Tequila inquired. "I'm getting tired of this, Bighead. We will take her alive to the gorge of Santa Helena Cañon and push her over. If someone ever does get down in those rapids to find her, there will be no bullet holes, no nothing. She just went too close to the edge, see?"

"How can you talk like this about the *pobrecita?*" asked Másomenos weakly from the rear. "After all, she is a *señorita, amigos.* Even you I have never seen kill a girl before."

"She saw us with those cattle," said Bighead. "Nobody ever saw me with wet cattle and lived to tell. How do you think I've kept my neck out of a rope this long? By advertising my work? *¡Punta en boca!*"

Másomenos shut his mouth, and the dust rose white around them as they increased their pace down the river road toward the gorge. They topped a rise and could look westward toward Oro Peso, drowsing brown and ancient in the sun, and then dropped down the other slope, and the milky mist of the rapids shredded above the gorge ahead. Elgera licked her lips, unable to keep her eyes from dropping to the big Remington at Bighead's hip. He hitched at it, grinning drunkenly. "Not this time, *Señorita* Scorpion."

It was the way he said the name. She could feel her legs begin to tremble against the saddle skirt from sheer tension, and a small, twitching pain caught beneath her shoulder blades. She tried to relax, but it was no good. The terrain was growing rugged here, uplifts thrusting up brokenly, limestone and lava poking through grassed-over slopes. The road wound down toward the upper end of the old Smuggler's Trail where it wound tortuously into the gorge. They reached the lip of the escarpment, and Bighead got his gun out, dismounting. He waved the Remington for the girl to get off La Rubia. Tequila's saddle creaked faintly as he swung down, a sardonic grin crossing his pockmarked face. The dull roar of the rapids came up to them, and Elgera could barely hear Másomenos behind her.

"Please, *amigos,* please, if you could only do it some other way. A *señorita* . . . a woman . . . I don't like it . . . !"

Bighead raised his voice to be heard clearly. "Will you walk over the edge yourself, *Señorita* Scorpion" — and, again, it was the way he said the name — "or do we have to help you?"

She looked down the black bore of his .44 and could sense Tequila's impatient movement to her side, and she was trembling once more, and it was not tension now. She tried to move, but was held rigid by her own infinite sense of helplessness. Bighead shrugged and began moving toward her with the gun. Elgera's head turned, looking desperately for a way out. Only Tequila was there, a gun in his hand, too, now, grinning that way, no mirth left in it, a little forced. Elgera felt pain in her hands and realized her fists had clamped shut so tightly her nails were drawing blood. Maybe it was Másomenos. Elgera did not know exactly. Somebody said it. Somebody said it when that figure appeared on the limestone split behind them, silhouetted for that moment against the sky, a man in a swirling cape sitting straight and tall on a black horse.

"*Madre de Dios*. El Morzillo. Penasco!"

Bighead turned, shouting something Elgera could not distinguish, and Tequila whirled that way, too. The first to recover, Elgera threw herself in among the horses while the three men were still staring at the rider. Tequila twitched toward her, snapping a shot, but she was already behind his dun, and the shot caught the horse instead. The animal reared up, whinnying shrilly, and plunged forward in a blind frenzy of pain. Tequila had to jump out of the way as it charged past him. Trying to keep the other two horses between her and the men, Elgera went into a stumbling run up the rocky hill. It was straight toward Penasco, but it was the only way out. Then, with her head turned upward, she realized the rider was no longer atop the uplift. There was more firing down below, and someone was shouting in pain, and she flung herself over the crest and down the other side. She tripped and fell and rolled down the rocky slope, ripping her silk shirt and her flesh alike, crackling through a spread of creosote, wet berries showering her face as she rolled through a clump of strawberry cactus, crying out as the spines stabbed her. She struck bottom and stumbled to her feet, shaking her head dazedly, tears streaming from her eyes with the stunned pain. The haze in this gully was thick and damp, and she groped blindly down the stony bottom of the cut. Someone had crossed the uplift before her. She saw him lying huddled ahead, one hand caught up in the branches of a mesquite bush that he must have grabbed at as he had fallen. Másomenos.

She was still crouching there by the fat man, staring at his dead, brown cheek, when she sensed the movement behind her. Tequila stood there with his gun in his hand.

"Did you think I wouldn't follow you over the hill?" he asked. Then he saw Másomenos. "Did you kill him?"

She stared up at Tequila without answering, her mouth open slightly, that strained look on her pale face. He came closer, frowning in a puzzled way. Then he was near enough to see what was stamped on Másomenos's cheek, and his voice came out in a husky whisper. *"La Rúbrica de Penasco."* His chest began to rise and fall perceptibly. "But we were never hooked up with Juárez. Hell, I was a little boy when it happened. And Másomenos. Why? We never crossed Penasco. We never even saw him." For the first time she saw fear in Tequila. All the sardonic humor was gone, and his voice took on a shrill babble. "He only kills those he has sworn vengeance on. Zaragosa, Guerrera. Not us. Not Másomenos. Not me. . . ."

She had recovered from the shock of it herself now, and she took a chance, while he was still shouting. Without rising from where she crouched, she shifted her weight to her left leg and kicked out with her other foot. It threw her over on her back, but the boot caught Tequila's wrist, knocking it upward. He cried out with the pain, his big Colt dropping from his fingers. She rolled over on the ground, clawing for the gun. Tequila's weight came down on top of Elgera with a force that knocked the breath from her in an exploding gasp. He caught her hand on the gun, striving to tear it free. She jerked out of his grasp and, in a final desperation, swung her arm, releasing the gun to fly in an arc over the body of Másomenos and land with a metallic clang on the stones, skidding across them down the gully. Elgera got over on her back and brought a knee into Tequila's groin, hearing his gasp of pain. For that instant his weight was limp on her, and she squirmed free, rising to her feet. He tried to catch at her feet, but she kicked free. Then she saw what made the haze so thick here. This gully opened out onto the escarpment forming the lip of the gorge, too, and the foam rising from the rapids below hung over the uplifts, viscid and milky. In their struggle, they had rolled past Másomenos and the gun, and, as Tequila scrambled to his feet, he came after Elgera without trying to find the weapon, anger stamped into his sweating face. She ran toward the open end of the gully, stumbling through torch cactus, kicking the stones from beneath her high heels, turning to see Tequila gaining on her. He must not have realized how near they were to the edge, or perhaps his anger blinded him to anything but getting his hands on her. With a garbled curse, he threw himself at Elgera.

His body, big and blurred before her, she let herself drop like a sack to one side. His foot caught her head as he went on over her.

"*¡Madre de Dios!*" he screamed, and then she could not hear him any more or see him.

She didn't look at the edge of the gorge as she got up. She didn't want to. She was barely on her feet, when the other man came on the run out of the gully and then slowed down as he saw her there, and then stopped.

"We won't make any mistakes about it this time," said Bighead, raising his gun. "We won't try to push you over." She saw his thumb draw the hammer back. "You just stand right where you are and I'll shoot you over!"

He had not wanted it this way. He had done the thing intelligently up to now. He had been El Cojo and had run his Cueva in Oro Peso, and he had waited patiently to hear of each man to whom he owed a debt. Guerrera, Zaragosa, all the others before them, and the others who would come after. Maybe there would be no others after now. He could not help it. It was no longer intelligence or cunning. It was the way he felt about the girl.

Cojo worked his way down through the crumbling strata of limestone, his *capuz*

229

torn by the torch cactus above, carrying one of the ivory-handled Frontier Colts with his *rúbrica* stamped into its butt, the other gun still holstered at his side. The ring of the Penascos was on his finger, the *rúbrica* itself wrought in steel with a fine cutting edge that would leave its mark irrevocably in the flesh of a man's face. Másomenos already bore that mark, lying dead back there in the mist.

In the confusion, Cojo had seen the fat man run blindly over the ridge, followed by the girl, and had dismounted from El Morzillo to go after them, finding Másomenos in the bottom of the gully. Cojo was possessed with the blinding rage that was so much a part of him, and he made no distinctions. All he knew was they were going to kill Elgera, and Másomenos was with them. Rarely did that rage control him; mostly it lay dormant in his scarred, twisted body, held down by the terrible grip of his will. But it was always there, black and malevolent, seething to erupt and consume him.

When he had found Parque Guerrera, for instance, on the Castellán Road, and all the old memories had come flooding up — the sight of his brother writhing on the *lanzas* of Guerrera's troops when they had come to confiscate the Penasco property for supporting Maximilian — the sight of his father falling dead before Guerrera's flaming *pistola*. It had been so easy to exact his vengeance.

Once he had found Zaragosa in the flats south of the Chisos Mountains, all the old pains had come flooding up, so vividly they made his bullet-riddled legs ache again where Zaragosa's slugs had smashed into them, so real he had felt the rope around his neck where Zaragosa had placed it with his own hands. It had been so easy to exact his vengeance.

And so it was now. All he knew was they were going to kill the girl, and that rage gripped him till he was trembling with it, and he had been able to kill Másomenos without the least compunction and stamp the *rúbrica* into his flesh for all to see what happened to those who crossed Real Penasco. After Másomenos, he moved up the gully, away from the gorge, thinking the girl had gone that way. When out of sight of the dead fat man, he had heard the sounds of struggle down there and had turned back. He was passing Másomenos again, hardly aware of him, going toward the gorge. Abruptly, out of the mist at the end of the gully, he heard someone shout.

"*¡Sacramento!*"

Stumbling across the stony bottom, Cojo

burst from the end of the gully with his gun held out in front of him, and the dim figure, standing at the edge of the gorge, was Elgera. But the pale blot of her face did not turn directly toward him, even as he appeared, and he whirled to one side, as the gun crashed from there. His short blue *capuz* twitched with the slug going through it.

Then the hammer of his Frontier dropped, and the gun bucked in his hand, and he saw Bighead take a step backward up the slope, surprise stamped onto his face, and then take a step forward, pain replacing the surprise, and then fall, and roll a little, and stop.

Cojo did not turn back to the girl, for there was another man coming up from the old Smuggler's Trail. He had dismounted by now — Chisos Owens — and he came in a heavy, purposeful walk that left no doubts as to his intent. He had that big Bisley in one fist, and his head raised a little when he saw Cojo.

"Chisos," called the girl, and the rising roar of the rapids below so muffled her voice that Cojo himself could hardly distinguish the words. "Chisos . . . don't. It's Cojo. Can't you see? He gave me the chance to get away, Chisos. He was only trying to stop

Bighead and Tequila. Please, Chisos."

But the big man had not heard her, and his steady walk carried him on toward Cojo inexorably. Cojo felt the muscles of his legs growing rigid beneath him, because he had fought this man before, and knew how much it would take to stop him. The girl was starting to run toward them from the lip of the gorge, and Cojo saw she meant to throw herself in front of him. Chisos shouted something at Elgera, and then broke into a run himself. Cojo spread his legs a little, and fired. Through the mist, he saw Chisos stagger slightly to one side, then reach out with his free left hand to grasp his gun, holding it in both hands, coming on.

"Chisos!" screamed Elgera, and threw herself in front of Cojo, holding onto his shoulders, her head twisted around toward the other man. But Chisos kept on coming with his gun held out in both hands.

Knowing a sudden fear for the girl, Cojo swept her aside, jumping out in front of her. He was jerking his gun into line again, when he saw the Bisley in Chisos's two big fists flame. It was like a hammer hitting Cojo's chest, and he knew why Bighead had taken that step back, as he himself stumbled backward, tripping over the girl's legs where he had thrown her to the ground, and he had known the same kind of pain when Zaragosa's bullets had swept his legs from beneath him, only this was a greater pain, and different, and, lying there on his back, he knew how different.

When Elgera realized Cojo was down, she got to her knees and crawled toward him. "Oh, Chisos, Chisos," she began to sob, "he wasn't going to kill me . . . don't you know that . . . he wasn't."

Chisos Owens had dropped his gun, now that it was all over, and he stumbled toward them, gripping his wounded right shoulder. "He's Penasco, isn't he?"

"Yes, but he wasn't going to kill me."

"Never mind, *chiquita*," said Cojo wearily. "He is right. I am Penasco, and he would have killed me wherever we met, whether I meant you harm or not. It is like Lupita said. I have been mostly bad. It is rather ironic, no, that my downfall should come as the result of what was probably the only good thing I ever did in my life? But at least I kept them from killing you."

"What happened to you?" she asked. "When Tequila went back with the fat man, you were gone."

"My horse had run off when I came to," he said. "I figured Bighead and Tequila would come across the river with you. I didn't know they meant to kill you here. I knew I could not catch them without a horse once they got across the Río, and the cave where I kept El Morzillo was closer than Oro Peso. I cut straight through the hills and must have passed you and the men while they were fooling around coming back to get me. Chisos was coming up the Smuggler's Trail when I got El Morzillo out, and forced me back up. It was then I topped the rise at the upper end of the trail and saw you and Tequila and Bighead." Cojo looked up at Chisos Owens. "You seemed surprised to see me, *señor*. I thought you recognized me last night on the ridge above Santa Helena flats."

"Is that why you tried to kill me?" asked Chisos.

Cojo nodded. "You can understand I did not want anyone to recognize me as Penasco."

"Your bullet missed my lung," said Chisos. "Elgera took me to Lupita's uncle down there below the ridge."

"I thought you were dead, Chisos." Elgera was biting her lip, eyes wet. "I saw Parco's house from the ridge and took you there. I wouldn't have left you, even then, but I had to get back to Oro Peso before daylight. I swore I'd get Penasco for killing you, and I knew the only way I could have an inside track was for Cojo to keep trusting me. I didn't know he was Penasco then. I only knew everybody came to his Cueva sooner or later."

"*Sí, sí. . . .*" Cojo tried to laugh, but choked on it, and could not speak for a moment. "Everybody comes to the Cueva sooner or later. That's why I was El Cojo. Oro Peso is the crossroads between Mexico and Texas, and sooner or later I would hear of every man I had sworn vengeance on. I heard Zaragosa had caught Tequila and was bringing him across the border by the Chisos foothills, and I found him that night just after Tequila had escaped."

"But Lupita must have known you were Penasco," said Chisos. "She came to her uncle's *jacal* and told me how to find where you kept El Morzillo."

Faint surprise showed in Cojo's dulling eyes. "Perhaps she followed me one night," he admitted finally, and then looked up at Chisos. "So she betrayed me." He shrugged. "That is a woman, *señor. Pues,* she was the only one who knew. Bighead and Tequila and the rest thought I was just El Cojo, The Lame One, running my Cueva for their nightly carousals and helping them with a little *Rurale* trouble occasionally because a man who runs a *cantina* on the border lasts longer if he does not antagonize the local bad boys." He was looking at Elgera now. "You see why I wanted you to go? . . . before you found out about me . . . while it was still clean and sweet between us, like the smell of spring grass. It was the only clean thing that ever happened to me, the only decent thing, and I wanted to keep it that way." He started to cough thickly again and fumbled beneath his *capuz*. "How about once more, Elgera. *Pronto,* eh? It has to be that way. Just once more. Cut me?"

He had taken the deck of cards out, and Elgera saw how little time there was left. "I'll shuffle," she said, taking the deck from his hands. Trying to see the cards through her tear-filled eyes, she spotted a two of clubs as it fluttered through her fingers and let her thumb nail catch at its top edge. He was watching her face, rather than her hands, and she slipped the deck into his hands for him to cut. He cut it and held it out to her. She let her sensitive index finger run across the edge of the deck, and the card she drew did not come from the top. Then he took one, turning it face up.

"Ten of hearts," he said faintly.

She turned hers face up. "Two of clubs."

"*Bueno,*" he murmured, "*bueno.*"

She bent her face to touch his smiling lips with hers.

After they had drawn the blue *capuz* across his somber face, Chisos and Elgera stood there, the big man trembling with weakness and reaction from his wounds. She held out her arms to support him, only now appreciating the incredible drive it must have taken to bring him out like this with a bullet wound that bad through his ribs.

"How did you really feel about Cojo?" he asked huskily.

"I don't know," she said, trying not to cry again. "I guess I won't know for a long time, Chisos. Maybe never. He wasn't all bad. He couldn't have been. He was decent to me. He was a murderer, and there's no justification for that, but who's to say we wouldn't do the same thing under circumstances like that, seeing our family killed, our land taken?" She looked up at him. "Do you think it was wrong?"

He frowned in a puzzled way, then he must have understood, for a faint smile caught at his lips. "The kiss? I don't think anybody would blame you. He saved your life, and it's like you say . . . he was just a poor tortured devil, all twisted up inside and out by what had happened to him. I don't think anybody would blame you."

"I don't know. I don't know," she said wearily. "It's all so mixed up inside of me. I still can't hate him or condemn him. I thought I hated Penasco when it looked like you were dead, but even that's gone now. I guess there's only one thing I do know."

There was a new tenderness in his hands on her. "One thing?"

"Yes," she said tiredly, "that's the first time in my life I ever cheated at cards."

The Shadow in Renegade Basin

It was in 1948 that Les Savage, Jr., began making his initial forays into the psychological Western story in ways previously attempted by only a few, preëminently Max Brand and Walter Van Tilburg Clark. It was with these stories that Savage would have a great impact on other Western writers just starting out. "The Shadow in Renegade Basin," which harks back to the spiritual terrain of Greek drama, was submitted by August Lenniger, Savage's agent at the time, to Fiction House under the title "Bushbuster" — which Savage's agent felt seemed more "Western" or, at least, more traditional than certainly was the story. Malcolm Reiss bought the novelette on May 4, 1948; but, once having it, he didn't know what to do with it. An author of Western fiction himself in the early 1930s, Reiss rewrote the ending to give it a ranch romance conclusion and finally published it in the Summer, 1950 issue of *Frontier Stories* under the title "Tombstones for Gringos." The themes of incest and fratricide were also modified. Yet, once they were, the Æeschylian notion of evil being visited upon generation after generation of a once great house was lost. It may also be worth noting, in regard to this tale, that one of the legends spun in Classical Antiquity about Teiresias, the blind seer who figures so prominently in Sophocles's Theban cycle of plays about Œdipus, is that his blindness was a punishment meted out to him by the goddess Athena for his once having looked upon her naked body while she was bathing. The fully restored text of this story first appeared in *The Western Story: A Chronological Treasury* (University of Nebraska Press, 1995) edited by Jon Tuska and has been issued by D H Audio in the compilation, *The Bold West*: Edition Twelve.

One

It was just one of the many mountains forming the Patagonias, a few miles north of the Mexican border, but something made it stand out from the other peaks — some singular, almost human quality of brooding, dominating malignancy. Its dome rose toward the sky, like a bare, scarred skull, and a line of stunted timber grew in a strange, scowling line across its brow. Some mineral in the land caused its shadow, settling across the basin, to have the deep, mordant tint of wet blood.

Colin Shane had halted his Studebaker wagon at the crest of Papago Divide to stare at the mountain, his deep-socketed eyes luminous with the growing spell of it. "Almost gives you the creeps, doesn't it?" he told his brother.

Farris Shane stirred on the wagon seat beside him, chuckling deeply in his chest. "You got too much of Ma's old Irish in you, Colin. All full of leprechauns and fairies."

"I heard a miner talking about it in Tombstone," said Colin. "El Renegado he called it. Some kind of legend connected with the mountain. When he heard we were planning to prove up on a homestead in Renegade Basin, he got a funny look on his face, and started his story. That was when you came in with word that Ma was worse. I wish we'd stayed to hear the story, now, somehow."

His face, turned somberly toward the south again, was not made for much humor, some Celtic ancestry lending the gaunt, bony structure of cheek and brow a countenance as dour and brooding as the mountain. His body was neatly coupled for such a long man, negligible through belly and hips, the only broad thing being his shoulders.

His younger brother beside him was in complete opposition, a short, heavy-chested replica of their father, with all the Red Irish of the man in his flaming hair and blue eyes. His thighs were so burly with bulging muscle they had split his jeans out along the seams, and his red flannel shirt was rolled to the elbows over heavy forearms, covered with hair as golded and curly as cured mesquite grass.

"You don't stop mooning, we'll never make the river by nightfall," he grinned.

Colin tried to shrug off his sense of oppression, turning to peer through the pucker of the Osnaburg sheeting covering the wagon. "You all right, Ma?"

Laura Shane's pain-wracked body stirred feebly beneath the blankets, within the stifling wagon. "Drive on, son. I'm still kickin'."

As Colin turned back, shaking the reins, a dim shout came from somewhere down the road. The tired horses drew them toward the sounds till the wagon rounded a turn in the road, and the words were intelligible.

"*Ai*, you *rumbero*, you are killing my birds. Nacho, *por Dios*, I have not revealed a thing. I am only a poor *pajarero*. . . ."

The horses came down off the grade and around a big rock, and Colin could see the two struggling men, among the bizarre, ridged shapes of tall saguaro. There were half a dozen bright-colored birds fluttering and squawking around in the air, scattering their feathers over the two men fighting in the sand, and half a dozen *amole* cages lying on the ground, some with their spindled doors torn open, three or four still holding shrieking parrots.

One of the men was a swarthy, thick-waisted Mexican in a fancy *charro* jacket and gleaming *mitaja* leggings. His immense sombrero had been torn off, and his long, black hair swung in greasy length down over his vivid, savage face, as he held the other man pushed down to his knees in the sand, beating at him — a greasy, fat little man with a pockmarked face and a red bulb for a nose, squirming and struggling to dodge the brutal blows.

"Let the little guy go, you big tub o' lard," shouted Farris, jumping off the wagon before it had stopped.

The squawking birds and rain of sand kicked up by the struggling men had excited the horses, and Colin was still fighting to halt them when Farris reached the Mexicans. He caught the bigger one by an arm, swinging him around to sink a vicious right fist in that thick waist. Colin had never seen a man before that Farris could not down with such a blow, but the Mexican only grunted harshly, taking a step backward and bringing both arms up to cover himself. Farris looked surprised, then plunged on in.

Colin had the horses halted by now, and jumped off the seat. The Mexican had already blocked Farris's next blow with his left arm, and was putting his own fist in under it. Farris staggered back, and the Mexican followed, hitting him again. This stiffened Farris. His face was white and working, and his whole body was lifted upward in a perfect, unprotected setup for the

Mexican, as he brought his third blow in, low to the belly.

"Meddling little *gringo*," he snarled, as he struck. Farris jackknifed at the waist over that fist. The Mexican stepped back and allowed him to fall.

At the same time Colin had reached them, charging in with all the long, close-coupled whiplash of him. He had seen how little effect his brother's blows had on the man and knew, if Farris could not do it that way, he couldn't, so he threw himself bodily at the Mexican's knees.

Legs pinned together by Colin's long arms, the man went over backwards, striking the ground heavily. Colin fought up across him to grab that long, greasy black hair, beating his head against the ground. They were in among the squawking, squalling birds now, with the fat little Mexican jumping around them and clapping his hands together.

"*Ai, ai,* that's it, beat the black Indian to a pulp! *¡Qué barbaridad!* If anyone deserves this, it is Nacho. What a bull you are, *señor. . . .*"

It was like trying to stun a rock. Nacho's face was twisted with the pain of the blows, but he still reached up with scarred, thick hands, pawing for Colin. Colin tried to

247

avoid them, sparring from side to side and beating that head again and again into the ground. Then one set of fingers caught on his arm, closed on it. He shouted aloud with the crushing pain. The other fist groped inexorably for his free hand, caught it, pulled him in. He squirmed spasmodically in the grip, appalled by the strength of the man beneath him. Like a bear, Nacho hugged him in, till his whole consciousness was popping and spinning in crushed pain.

"Hang on a minute, Colin, boy," he heard from somewhere behind him.

Colin opened his mouth as wide as he could, sunk his teeth into the nose beneath him. There was a deafening howl of pain, a spasm of wild thrashing. He hung on desperately. Neither would Nacho loosen his bear hug. He settled back, breathing through his mouth in a guttural, savage way, and began applying pressure once more.

Colin thought his lungs would burst. Ribs began to snap and crack. A terrible, maddening suffocation gripped him. Then he heard the sound. A dull, solid, whacking sound. Once. Twice. Three times. Suddenly the arms fell limply from around him. He lay a long time, sprawled across the body, gasping like a fish cast upon the land.

Finally he lifted his head to see Farris standing weakly above them, leaning on the spare wagon tongue he had unleashed from beneath the Studebaker.

"Couldn't do much more," he panted. "My guts are all stove in. Never saw a man with that kind of punch."

Colin got to his feet, slowly. The little Mexican was scrambling around among the cages, righting them and slipping the raucous birds back into them, a comical, pathetic little figure in an archaic, hooded cloak and red Turkish trousers that ballooned out around the ankles.

"Come here, Pepita," he called to one of the birds perched on a saguaro. "Come little one, back to your cage. He is a macaw, *señores*, from the land of the white Indians, in Darien. And Roblero there . . . come, Roblero, your castle awaits . . . Roblero is a white-necked raven. He even talks. Say something, Roblero."

"*Qué un rumbero,*" squawked the raven.

"We know all your birds now," said Colin. "How about you?"

"Ah," the little man cackled, turning toward them with a sly, upraised finger. "I am Pajarero. It means bird-catcher, *señores*. You must have seen us in Tintown. The place is made up of bird-catchers. Would you like to buy this tanager? Only three *pesos*. A rare bird, *señores*."

"As rare as this one on the ground?" said Farris, turning his pale eyes to Nacho, who was beginning to regain consciousness now.

The sly humor left Pajarero as his eyes dropped to Nacho. He made the sign of a cross before himself as Nacho rolled over, lifting himself painfully to his hands and knees. Shaking his head, he looked up at Colin, and the intent was plain in his smoldering eyes.

"Do anything more and I'll clout you again!" growled Farris, moving in with the wagon tongue.

Nacho rose to his feet. His hand opened and closed above the butt of his holstered gun, but Farris could have struck him again before he got it free.

"There are many more days left in the year, *señores*," he said at last, and turned to walk out among the saguaros. Colin expected him to get out of range of that wagon tongue and then turn back, going for his gun. He took a breath that swelled his flat belly against the barrel of his own gun, stuck naked through his belt, just behind the buckle, and waited that way, to pull at it if Nacho turned. But the man disappeared among the tall, haunted cactus without wheeling back.

"You had better leave the basin before another of those days comes," said Pajarero, at last. "I have heard him say that to seven men. They are all dead now."

"We don't scare that easy," said Colin. "We aim to prove up on some government land here. We couldn't go on if we wanted. We're out of money, and Ma's too sick. I don't even think the horses could pull another mile."

"Homesteading . . . here?" said Pajarero, in an awed voice.

"What's wrong with here?" asked Farris.

"You have not heard about . . . El Renegado?"

"The mountain?" Colin asked him. "What about it?"

"Ooh . . . ," the man pouted his lips, pulling his fat head into his shoulders, "perhaps I had better not tell you."

Farris shifted his weight, with that wagon tongue. "Perhaps you had. I'm tired of all this mystery."

"Very well, *señor,* very well," said the man hastily. The pout faded from him as he turned toward the mountain. "Do you see how empty the valley is? Not a house, not a man. The richest basin in this area, more water, more grass, more everything than you could find within a hundred miles. Open to homesteading many months now. Yet not a house, not a man."

"Yes?" said Farris cynically.

"It is said," murmured Pajarero, turning back to him, "that anyone who settles in the shadow of El Renegado is doomed."

Two 🦅

The two brothers made camp that evening in the rich river bottom. Colin cut willow shoots for his mother's bed, laying them herring-bone to make a light, springy mattress. Farris found fresh meat in a mule deer back in the hills, and they had that and sourdough for supper. The Mexican bird-catcher had come with them, and ate sparingly as his feathered charges, for all his corpulence, regaling them with fabulous stories of his wanderings in search of birds. Farris's cynicism had kept him from elaborating upon what he had said about the mountain, and it was not until after supper that it was again brought to Colin's attention. Laura Shane did it. She had eaten little and was feverish, and, as Colin sat by her bed, she caught at his wrist with one veined, bony hand.

"I heard what that Mexican said this afternoon," she moaned. "He was right, Colin. Don't settle here. The land is cursed. I can feel it."

"Don't let your Irish blood get the best of you, Ma," soothed Farris. "The land's no more cursed than we are, just because we've been plagued with a little bad luck these last years."

"You're the practical one, Farris," muttered their mother. "Too much like your father. If you can't put your hands to a thing, it don't exist. It does for Colin. He knows what I mean. Don't stop here, Colin. . . ."

"We've got to, Ma," Colin told her. "It's our last chance. You know that. . . ."

He had meant to say more, but it would not come. There was a figure in the firelight to stop him. He did not know exactly how she had gotten there. A woman. The dark, haunted face of a woman, tawny, dusky flesh and great black eyes that reflected the firelight opaquely. It was hard to separate her black hair from the night behind her. There was a jet rosary at the swell of her breast, immense black pearls and silver bracelets on her slender wrists.

Pajarero had risen from the fire, staring at her with wide, liquid eyes, gripped in some strange enchantment. Colin felt the same way, unable to speak. It had always been Farris who had been easy with the women anyway, grinning confidently, now, and wrapping his tongue around the blarney.

"Well, an angel stepped right out of heaven . . . how can the basin be cursed when they grow such beautiful flowers here, a little bit o' colleen wrapped up in Spanish lace and called *señorita*. We're the Shanes. I'm Farris, my brother Colin, and our mother, Laura."

"I am Cristina Velasco," the woman murmured, her English accented just enough to give her husky voice a tenuous, piquant appeal. "My *hacienda* is on the other side of the basin. I heard your mother was ill. I wondered if I could help."

"With the gratitude of Erin to greet you," smiled Farris, holding out his hand. Colin could see the little lights kindling in his eyes, as they played over her body. She allowed the redhead to guide her over the rough, matted ground toward Laura Shane, but halted momentarily before Colin.

"You have not spoken," she said.

"When my boy has anything worth saying," Laura Shane said, from her sickbed, "he'll speak."

Cristina Velasco inclined her head to one side in a thoughtful, studying way, smiling faintly at Colin. Then she moved on, passing Pajarero. He had been staring at her all the while with those shining eyes and faintly parted lips. She nodded at him in a gracious, dimly condescending way as she passed. A shudder seemed to travel through his whole body.

"Señorita," he whispered, dropping to his knees and reaching out one hand, as if to grasp the hem of her skirt and kiss it. But she pulled it up at that instant to avoid a hummock of dirty grass, and he drew his hand back sharply, a strange, apologetic line rounding his shoulders.

The woman knelt beside Laura Shane and spoke on a sharp, disgusted little exhalation. "You are letting her drink this water? How stupid. That's the first thing you should have stopped. Even boiling it does not help the newcomer to the valley. There is some wine in my *carroza*. Please get it for me?"

The tilt of her head indicated the road, and Colin started off through the willows. He found the *carroza* to be an old Spanish coach, parked alongside the road. A man rose from where he had been squatting against the high back wheel, smoking a cigarette. He looked Indian, with a round, enigmatic face and sullen eyes, his smooth wrists tinkling with turquoise and silver jewelry.

"*Señorita* Velasco sent me to get some wine," Colin said.

The man nodded, opened the door, bent inside to get a clay jar. He handed it to Colin without speaking, and squatted back against the wheel, staring at Colin with unwinking eyes. Colin wended his way back through the matted undergrowth of these rich bottomlands to their camp. Cristina was still kneeling beside his mother, washing her face now and murmuring Spanish in an unintelligible, soothing way.

"She's so feverish," she told Colin, reverting to English.

"You don't need to talk Yankee if you don't want," Colin told her in Spanish. "We were raised on the Texas border before we hit for Missouri."

She looked up in surprise, then asked him: "Have you anything for her?"

"The doc in Tombstone gave us some Dover's powder."

The woman made a disgusted sound, picking up her skirts as she rose, and headed for the undergrowth. Colin followed her in puzzlement. He found Pajarero at his heels, staring after the woman with that dog-like devotion. She called for a torch, and Farris thrust a length of sappy wood into the fire, bringing the light to her. In a few moments she had collected what looked like a bunch of common weeds, carrying them back to the fire in her skirts.

In amazement, Colin watched her slender, aristocratic hands go about the work with such skill. She labored for hours with his mother, feeding her the romero tea, performing the mysterious, amazing healing arts of these border people, learned slowly, painfully, through the long centuries when there was no doctor within a thousand miles. They were all dozing about the fire when Laura finally became quieter, drifting off into a troubled sleep. Cristina rose from her side, waking Colin with the movement. He got up unsteadily, gazing at his mother.

"That's the first real sleep she's had in weeks," he said.

"It is well," said Cristina. "She will feel more like traveling in the morning. You must bring her to my *hacienda* for a few days before you leave the valley."

"We aren't leaving the valley," Colin told her.

She whirled on him, a strange, wild look obliterating the almost Oriental calm of her face for a moment, then disappearing as violently as it had come, wiped away by some inward effort of her own. "You can't stay," she said intensely.

"You're not talking about the mountain?" he asked.

"How can you think of staying, if you know?"

"I don't know," he said. "Pajarero started to tell us, but he closed up tight when Farris scoffed at him. What is it?"

She stared up at his eyes in a fixed, fascinated way, held by the rapport the sincerity of his voice brought. She started to smile; then, it faded before a puzzled frown that drew her brows together. She began, haltingly at first, her voice gaining conviction at the quiet attention on his face.

"When Don Juan Oñate first made his conquest of this country," she said, "he established a *presidio* in this basin, with a priest for the mission, and a company of Spanish soldiers and their families. Commanding them was a young captain who fell in love with an Indian girl belonging to the tribe in the Patagonias. These Indians were so war-like that the priest had only converted a few of them, who were working in the mission as neophytes. The others planned to wipe out the *presidio*. Through his contact with the woman, the captain knew this, and could have saved his comrades. But he betrayed them, running off to the mountain with the woman. He was called El Renegado, and the mountain came to be named after him.

"The attack came near evening, when the shadow of the mountain touched the *presidio*. It was the changing of the guards, and with help from the neophytes inside the Indians overwhelmed the garrison and wiped them out, women and children and all. The priest was mortally wounded, but, before he died, he declared the ground touched by the shadow of the mountain to be cursed by the death of so many innocents. The basin is so shaped that all of it, during the course of the day, is touched by that shadow, and there is not one person to try and settle here who has not been blighted by that curse."

"Why are you here, then?" he asked.

She turned sharply away from him, as if to hide the subtle alterations hardening her face. "Because I am," she answered finally, and then lifted her chin toward the east, dawn light making a cameo of her face. "The sun will be up in a few minutes. If you will wake your mother, I will go and prepare the coach for her. It will be more comfortable to her than that wagon."

He walked over to kneel by his mother, taking her shoulder gently. It felt cold. He shook her lightly. Her body reacted with the lifeless motion of a rag doll. He bent down to stare at her face. There was no sign of breathing. He gazed for a long, blank moment at her closed eyes, conscious of Farris's rising from the fire, to come over by him.

"I guess you won't have to get the coach

ready," he told Cristina at last. "Mother's dead."

At that moment, the sun lifted its first brazen rays above the undulating silhouette of the mountains to the east. But its brightness did not seem to touch them here. Colin realized why. The bulk of the sun lay behind the ugly, brooding peak of El Renegado, throwing its shadow across the valley, to shroud their whole camp.

☙ Three

There was not much will for living left in either of the brothers for several weeks after their mother's death. They buried her on a hill above the camp they had made in the bottoms, and remained there, hunting and fishing for the food they needed. It was Farris who seemed to recover first, finally coming up with the suggestion that they build a house. This hard work helped to take their minds off their mother's death.

After they had built a three-room adobe and some corrals, they made a trip north, over Papago Gap, trading some of their meager household goods from Missouri for onions and chiles from the Mexican *pajareros* in Tintown. And farther north, among the Papagos and Pimas, they found one butcher knife was worth a wagon load of melons and squash and Indian corn for seed crops. They got half a dozen peach and apricot trees to transplant about their house, and the fruit was beginning to ripen by June. And then it was that evening when Colin stood out among those trees, enjoying a cooling breeze after the heat of the late spring day, seeking satisfaction in what they had built here.

He did not find as much as he sought. He wondered if his mother's death was still too recent. Or was it something else? Farris came up behind him, smoking his pipe.

"You got Tina on your mind?" he asked.

"What makes you say that?" smiled Colin.

"You're looking off toward her place."

"Seems to me you're the one who should have her on your mind," Colin told him. "You've gone to see her every Saturday we've been here."

"You might as well have come along," chuckled Farris. "Seems all we talked about was you. Makes me jealous, she's so interested. Wanted to know why you didn't call. I told her you was shy with women."

"What did she say?"

"She said she didn't think that was true . . . you just moved a little slower than me, and didn't say anything until you could really mean it."

"I should think so," said Colin, with one of his rare, fleeting smiles. "With all your blarney." He sobered. "I guess I was thinking about her, in a way, Farris. We've got the house to a place where it needs a woman."

"The same thought's been in my mind," Farris murmured.

Colin turned to look at his brother in some surprise, and Farris chuckled, poking the pipe at him. "We aren't going to be in competition, are we, Colin?"

For a moment, Colin wanted to answer it with a grin, but he could not. When it finally came, it was forced. "What chance would I stand, against a lady's man such as your-self . . . ?"

He stopped speaking to stare out at something beyond. The earth beneath him seemed to be trembling. Then there was the sound. A great, growing sound.

"Earthquake?" asked Farris, stiffening.

"Stampede!" cried Colin, with the first bawl of cattle reaching him. "Those black-horns up the valley. Get your horse, Farris! If they come through our fields, we'll lose everything."

Their stock was fat, now, from the rich graze of the valley, moving restlessly in the pack-pole pen behind their corral. Colin hooked a bridle from the top pole and swung the gate open, jamming it in the first mouth he found, swinging aboard without waiting for a saddle. It was one of the bays they had used in the wagon team, a good enough horse for this short run.

Colin raced out through their new orchard and across the alfalfa on this side of the river. On the opposite bank he could see them now, a milling, bawling herd of blackhorns, trampling through the Indian corn just thrusting its tender green shoots from the soil.

"Keep them on that side or they'll ruin our alfalfa, too," shouted Farris, coming up from behind Colin on another animal, and both of them plunged into the ford toward the cattle. It did not look like a stampede to Colin. The cattle were headed in no definite direction as yet. They seemed to have milled in the cornfields, and now were being shoved unwillingly into the river by some unseen pressure.

Before the brothers were halfway across the broad, shallow ford, however, the leaders of the herd were plunging into the water. More and more cattle followed, and their direction was becoming more definite. Colin started shouting hoarsely in an effort to turn them back. The leaders spooked at his loud voice and oncoming horse, trying to turn aside, but there were too many behind them.

The true charge began with a burst, as the whole front rank seemed to break into a deliberate charge at Colin, bawling and screaming in the stupid, bovine frenzy that would carry them blindly forward when the primeval fright of the stampede finally reached them.

"Get out of he way, Colin!" yelled Farris, from behind. "You can't stop them now. They'll run you down. . . ."

Colin only half heard him, urging his own spooked mount on ahead, in a deep, black anger that so many months' work could be wiped out in a few minutes. He was into the leaders, then, still screaming at them in an effort to start a mill. But their impetus carried his horse back on its haunches. The beast tried to turn and run with them. It stumbled on the rough bottom, and began lunging from side to side, squealing, losing its head entirely. Colin realized he would go down in another moment.

Halfway between the bank and the herd, Farris had started to turn his horse aside. When he saw what had happened to Colin, he wheeled the animal around and raced straight for the herd.

"Get back, you fool!" Colin screamed at him. "You'll only get killed, too."

But Farris plunged right on toward him. Colin had managed to rein his horse around in the direction of the cattle, but he was pinched in between two of the leaders now, and the animal had not yet found its footing. He felt it stumble again, heavily, and knew, with the knowledge born of a lifetime on horseback, that this time it was going down for good. Farris must have seen it, too, for just as he reached the head of the herd, he wheeled his horse broadside, shouting at Colin to jump for it.

A dozen feet separated them. Colin lunged upward on his foundering, falling horse, got purchase enough with one heel on its off flank to kick away, and jumped. He struck the side of a steer, caromed off, hit shallow water with both flailing feet. He ran three stumbling steps before the impetus of his jump robbed him of balance completely. The tail of Farris's horse was before his eyes as he went over. Blindly he clawed at it. He heard Farris shout, and felt the animal lunge forward under a kidney kick. It almost tore the tail from his hands, his arms from their sockets. He had a dim, vivid sense of little, bloodshot eyes and waving, tossing horns and churning legs, and realized Farris was running down the front ranks of the herd in a diagonal line, attempting to get out to the side before his own horse was caught up in them. The ford fell into deeper water, and then the tail was torn from Colin's hands as the horse stumbled and lost its feet, too.

He went under in a plummeting force, striking bottom, kicking off. He came to the surface, gasping for air, getting water instead, doubling over in a paroxysm of coughing that would have put him under again. He was too dizzy and disorganized to find control. But as he went down, panic paralyzing him, he felt a hand on his hair. He fought wildly, losing all sense in the terrible, primal fear of being drowned. There was a cracking blow against his jaw, and he seemed to sink into the delicious coolness of the deepest water. . . .

His next sensation was of gritty sand, and a muttering, a distant sound. He opened his eyes, tasting silt, coughing up a quart of water, before he saw Farris hunkered above him. He lay back, swearing at his brother affectionately.

"Damn' fool. I ought to pin your ears back. You could have gotten killed."

"You *would* have," grinned Farris. "It makes us even for the time you pulled Nacho off me."

"Let's not start keeping score," said Colin, sitting up. "I couldn't count high enough for the tight spots you've pulled me out of."

He stopped talking to stare after that muttering, dying sound of stampeding cattle running across the valley. Before his eyes lay the trampled, ruined alfalfa fields, the little grove of transplanted trees uprooted and mangled, the ocotillo corrals wrecked beyond repair and all the animals in them stampeded off with the beef. Then, somehow, his attention was not on that. It was beyond, climbing the steep, scowling slope of that scar of timber forming a frowning brow, and, above, to the somber, brooding dome of El Renegado, dominating the valley, and the night, with its malignancy.

🔫 Four

There was nothing they could do that night but try and get some sleep. The house was still intact, although one wall had been knocked in. When Colin awoke the next morning, Farris was not there. The redhead's guns were not in evidence, either, and Colin decided Farris had gone hunting.

Colin spent the morning searching the river bottom for their horses. He found the bay he had ridden, up on the bank where it had dragged itself to die with both front legs broken, and shot the hapless beast to put it out of its misery. Near noon he found the one Farris had forked, three miles downstream where it had been swept by the river. It was calmly cropping grama and was sound enough to ride.

Colin returned to find Farris still gone. He put a saddle on the horse and started tracking his brother. He found fresh sign leading out across the river into the hills behind them. Within these foothills he came across other sign mixed with Farris's footprints, the mark of hoofs, shod and unshod.

He lost them in the general trampling the herd had made here and was still trying to unravel it all when he sighted Farris, hiking back down a rocky slope toward him. His face was so covered with alkali it looked like a death mask, and even this could not hide the strange expression on it. He did not seem to see Colin till he was close, and only then did he make an effort to change the look.

"What is it?" said Colin.

"Nothing. Been hunting. Nothing up there."

"Horses mixed in with those cattle tracks," said Colin. "A shod one in with the unshod. What is it, Farris? Why won't you tell me?"

"There's nothing to tell." The redhead's voice was lifted shrilly. "Now let's get back."

Colin reined the horse around to block his brother's move to leave, one leg coming against the thick, sweating chest of him. He bent forward to peer at Farris. "You went up to the woman's place last Saturday."

"What makes you say that?" said Farris angrily.

"You don't get that slicked up to irrigate our corn."

"All right," said Farris. "So I went up to the woman's place. What's that got to do with it?"

"That's what I'd like to know," said Colin. "What's that got to do with this?"

The redhead's alkali-whitened face lifted in a sharp, strained way, and that same expression flitted through his eyes. "Listen, Colin," he said tightly, "quit swinging the horse around and let me by, will you? I been on a long hike and I'm tired and my temper won't stand all this blather."

"Tell me what you found and I'll let you past."

"Nothing, damn you, I told you. . . ."

"It's got something to do with her. You're shielding her!"

"The hell I am. You know. . . ." Farris halted himself with an effort so great it twisted his face. He stood there for a space that had no measure, chest rising and falling against Colin's leg, dampening it with sweat. Finally Farris reached up to fold his fingers around the stirrup leather, speaking in a grating restraint. "Listen, Colin, you and I have had our spats in the past, but this is different. I don't want to fight with you this way so soon after Mother's death. Or any other time, for that matter. Leave the woman out of it, will you?"

Colin had quieted for this moment, too, and the rapport they had known before was between them. He stared deeply into

Farris's pale blue eyes. "You really got a case on Tina, haven't you?"

"Colin," said Farris. "I think I'd kill the man who tampered with her . . . in any way."

Colin drew a deep breath. "Then I won't ask you what you found up there, Farris. Let go and I'll find out for myself."

"No." A tortured look passed through the redhead's face. "Please, Colin, there's nothing up there. . . ."

"Then why are you so bent on my not seeing it?" said Colin. "Let go, Farris."

"No."

"Farris" — there was a deadly, final quality to the tone of Colin's voice, startling after their rising shouts — "I'll ask you once more. Let me go."

"Only if you turn around and come home with me."

Colin snapped his foot from the stirrup, shoved it against Farris's chest with the leg jackknifed, straightened that long, lashing leg with a vicious force. Farris went over backward with a shout, hand torn loose of the stirrup leather. Colin slipped his foot back into the oxbow and booted the animal forward. He heard Farris call his name, but did not turn around, and then he was over the crest and into the next shallow valley.

Each great, ruddy rock clung hatefully to

its rough slope, scowling down upon Colin like some crouching, mordant demon. The scar of timber forming its brow was shadowed darkly, ominously, with no sign of life breaking the spell. Above timberline, the bald, lithic head thrust the seamed, scarred planes of its skull ominously toward the sky, like Lucifer defying St. Michael and all the angels.

Irish inheritance of a deep mysticism gave Colin an acute sensitivity to such influences, and he pushed forward without trying to laugh away the real, tangible sense of awe, almost of fear, the mountain engendered in him. He did not try to cross its crest, but pushed inward on the mountains behind by rounding its slope beneath the timber. Following Farris's tracks, he at last realized he was on some kind of trail leading through endless tiers of varicolored rocks. They blocked off sight of the valley behind him now. The air up here was stifling. His clothes were drenched with sweat. It seemed difficult to breathe, somehow. He kept glancing up at the mountain, as if seeking the cause in its malignancy. Then it spoke to him.

"*¿Qué pasa?*" it said, in a voice like the rustle of quaking aspens.

Colin halted his horse, shivering with the

shock of it. He keened up his head toward the sound. It was not the mountain. It was a man, sitting on a rock above the narrow trail, grinning down on him.

Colin did not think he had ever seen such age. The man's face was no more than a skull with parchment for skin, stretched so tightly the bones appeared ready to come through. The eyes stared, huge and feverish, from the gaunt coign of their sockets. The flesh of the hands was wrinkled and seamed, burned the color of ancient mahogany by the countless years of this land's sunshine, and the fingers shook with palsy on the butt plate of the ancient rifle that looked like the matchlock Colin's father had hung above the mantle in Missouri.

"You are one of Captain Velasco's men?" asked the ancient, in a strange, stilted Castilian. "Is he coming today?"

"I'm Colin Shane," Colin told him in Spanish. "Who are you?"

"Shane?" The man bent forward in senile belligerence, repeating the name in a shrill, suspicious way. "Shane? Shane? No one by that name with the captain. I've been waiting a long time. They say Don Oñate will be here soon. Did you see the inventory Captain Velasco made of his clothing? A true *conquistadore*. They say he has garters with points of gold lace in colors to match each costume. And doublets of royal lion skin. Do you believe that? Six pairs of Rouen linen shirts. Why should a man have that many? He can only wear one shirt at a time. Shane." He seemed to snap back with a jolt. "Shane?" He bent forward again. "Are you one of the Indians?"

"I come from the valley," said Colin, staring at the old man, trying to find mockery in him. There was a weird, sardonic light to those old eyes, a secretive leer on his lips. Or had the sun done this? Then he made out what it was beside the old man. An ancient, rusted Spanish helmet, and a cuirass of tarnished metal, backed with rotting leather that was still damp with sweat.

There was something dream-like about it — the strange costume, the archaic dialect, talk of men so long dead — but the harsh reality of it was brought home to Colin by the lighted match in the man's hand. His own response came automatically, a sudden move to rein the horse away, halted by the flick of the old man's hand toward the touch hole. Colin stared down the immense bore of that ancient gun, unwilling to believe that it could still fire, yet held stony by the possibility of it.

The old man bent toward him, cackling.

"I told him no more would come up from the valley. Fray Escobar's curse is useless. We're still alive, aren't we? And you die. One by one, you die. Even the don himself will not escape alive. Velasco is master here. El Renegado is king."

"Don't bring that match any closer, you fool," said Colin, trying to keep his voice level. "I'm not with Oñate. I'm an Irishman. Shane. Does that sound Spanish? I'm not your enemy."

"That's what the last one told me, and I let him by. He said he was an Indian bird-catcher from Tintown. Captain Velasco was in a great rage. He followed him out and killed him. He would have killed me, if I wasn't such a faithful friend. Oh, no. Not this time. I'll kill you this time."

That ghastly cackle rang against the rocks. Colin stared at the lowering match, filled with an awesome helplessness. He gathered himself for a last, desperate effort, meaning to wheel his horse and drop off the side at the same time. The tension filled him till he thought he would burst, and the match reached the touch hole.

"Stop it, *Cabo!*"

It was a clear, cutting voice, from above in the rocks. The old man jerked the match away with a surprised moan. Powder in the touch hole hissed, went out. Colin stared at the gun, trembling all over, and, for the first time, he felt the clammy sweat sticking his shirt to him. Finally he found himself staring upward. Cristina Velasco sat a black horse with four white stockings on a huge rock fifty feet above them. She was moving it now, bringing it carefully, delicately down some narrow trail Colin could not see. Colin had not seen a woman in pants too often. They were *charro*, of red suede, tight fitting as another layer of skin, and he could not help staring. She had a *charro* jacket, too, with gold frogs embroidered across the lapels against which her breasts surged. There was a strange, dark look to her face, almost an anger, as she reached their level. Colin could not tell if it was directed at him or the old man.

"*Cabo*," she said. "Go back, now."

"But Captain Velasco told me to. . . ."

"I told you to go back," she said, sharply. "You're relieved."

"It's about time," muttered the old man, gathering up his armor. "Seems like I've been out here for years."

"You have, you old fool," muttered Tina, too low for his ears. She waited till he had hobbled on up the trail and out of sight among the rocks, then turned to Colin. He

278

was watching her with a strange mixture of suspicion, and something else he could not define.

"*Cabo,*" he said. "Corporal?"

"The sun of this country can addle the brain, Colin," she said. "He is only a crazy old man who thinks he is back in the Sixteenth Century with Don Juan Oñate."

"And Captain Velasco?" said Colin.

She shrugged. "All right."

"You didn't tell me you were descended from him."

"Just because my name is the same?"

"Are you?"

"All right," she said, in a sudden anger. "So I am descended. And so I didn't tell you. It isn't something one goes around bragging about. He was a traitor, a murderer, a renegade, and all his descendants. . . ."

She cut off sharply, and his black brows raised as he asked her: "All his descendants what?"

"Nothing," she said, shaking her head sharply. "This is no place to talk. My *hacienda* is lonely. Will you join me in afternoon chocolate?"

They turned their horses down the slope, and she did not speak again till they were out of the rocks and into timber once more.

Then he found her eyes on him, studying his face.

"What were you doing up there?" she asked.

"A herd of cattle stampeded across our land last night," he told her. "Ruined most of our crops for this year. We found some horse tracks mixed in with the cattle sign this morning. Farris found something up here, but he wouldn't tell me what."

Perhaps it was the expression in his eyes looking at her, for she lifted her body in the saddle. "So you think I've taken to stampeding cattle now?"

"I didn't say that."

"You might as well."

"All right," he said. "What *are* you doing up here?"

"I . . . I . . . ," she broke off, biting her lip, eyes dropping. She shrugged. "You wouldn't believe me anyway."

"Yes, I would, Tina," he said. "Tell me one straight thing and I'll believe you."

Those big eyes raised again, gratefully. "I can see the mountain from my *hacienda*. I saw you come up here and thought you might run into The Corporal. He's old and he's crazy, but he can be dangerous. I didn't want you hurt, Colin."

He inclined his head. "I'm sorry. I guess I

should be thankful instead of suspicious. My apologies."

"That makes me feel much better," she smiled, and drew her horse over to lean towards him. "Now, if you will wipe that scowl off your face and come down to the house, perhaps you and I together can clear up just how you feel about me."

 # Five

It had once been a magnificent, extensive *hacienda,* with a high adobe wall surrounding an acre of buildings and corrals, but much of the wall was fallen in now, and all but one of the patios was overgrown with yucca and grama. They rode through a great gate into this one garden, where a stream gurgled through a little red-roofed well, and peach trees dropped their delicate bloom across the sun-baked tile topping the wall. The Indian Colin had found by the coach that first night appeared through a spindled door and took their horses.

Smiling, the woman whipped dust from her *charro* pants with a quirt, and turned to walk toward a cane chair by a long table. Colin started to follow her, and it was then they saw the man.

He had been standing in the deep shade of the wall, smoking a cigarette, and Colin had the sense of eyes being on them all the time, in that sly malevolence.

"Nacho!" The woman's voice held whispered shock.

He smiled, pinching out the cigarette and dropping it to grind the butt into the earth with his heel. With a thumb, he pushed the brim of his sombrero upward till the hat was tilted back on his head at a rakish angle. Then he hooked his hands in the heavy gun belt at his waist, and moved toward them in an unhurried, swaggering way, the chains on his great Mexican cartwheel spurs tinkling softly with each step.

"You consort with the *gringo* now," he told the woman.

"In my house, Americans are no more *gringos* than Mexicans are greasers," she said.

"*Your* house?" Nacho asked, brows raising in that mocking smile. Only then did he condescend to move his eyes to Colin. "Is this the day, *señor?*"

Remembering what the man had said that first time, Colin lowered his head a little. "Any day you want."

"I'm glad you leave the choice to me," smiled the man. "You will not wait long, *señor.*" He turned to the woman. "I want to speak with you."

"You would ask me to leave my guest?"

"Not asking you . . . telling you."

"Whatever you want to say can be said right here," she told him.

Those spur chains tinkled again. His movement forward was so fast Colin could not follow it till the man had grasped Tina by the wrist. She tried to pull away. Colin saw Nacho's knuckles go white. Tina's face contorted with the pain of the squeezing grip. She lifted the quirt to lash it across Nacho's face. He shouted with the stinging pain, and it allowed her to tear loose, stumbling backward across the garden. Tears squeezed from his squinting eyes as Nacho started after her. At the same moment, the Indian appeared once more through the spindled gate. He stopped, however, just within, making no move to stop Nacho. Colin spoke then.

"Nacho."

Again, the utter, deadly quiet of his voice had a startling effect after all the violence and noise. It stopped both Nacho and the woman. Nacho turned back his way. Colin was standing perfectly straight, with no inclination of body or arm to advertise his intent, yet Nacho's eyes flickered momentarily across the stag butt of the big Paterson thrust through Colin's belt just behind the buckle.

"*¿Sí, señor?*" Nacho said, in that mocking tone.

"Get out of this garden," said Colin.

"Now, *señor?*" asked Nacho.

"I won't ask you again," said Colin.

"You won't have to," said Nacho. His draw was as blinding as the rest of his movements. He halted it so abruptly his whole body shuddered. His gun was only halfway out of his holster, and he held it there with a tense, bent arm, staring in unveiled surprise at the Paterson filling Colin's hand, pointed at the middle of his belly.

The Indian had started some overt move, too, over there by the spindled gate, and stopped it as quickly as Nacho, with sight of Colin's weapon. Tina let out a small, moaning sound. Nacho allowed his gun to slip back in its holster, raising his eyes to Colin.

"Get out and on your horse," said Colin. "I'll be watching you out of sight. And I'll have this in my hand all the way."

"There are still enough days left in the year, *señor,*" said Nacho softly. He met Colin's gaze for a moment longer, his own eyes showing no particular defeat, smoldering with the banked coals of that subterranean hate. Then he turned, chains tinkling as he walked to the *zaguán.* He moved through the large gate and disappeared for a moment. They could hear the creak of saddle leather. Then he appeared again, spurring his horse cruelly into a headlong run. Colin inclined his head at the Indian.

"How about you?"

"That's all, Ichahi," said the woman.

The Indian let those enigmatic eyes pass over Colin as he turned to go.

Tina's glance followed Colin's movement as he thrust the Paterson back into his belt. Then she raised her eyes to his face, a new measure of him in their depths. "I would not have taken you for a gunfighter," she said.

"I'm not," said Colin. "Dad always said a man had no right to use tools unless he could use them well."

A mingling of emotions brought a subtle, indefinable change to her face, and then left it with only a strange, withdrawn calculation. She walked over to sit on the long, comfortable bench beneath a peach tree. She toyed idly with a ring on her middle finger, pouting a little. Feeling awkward, standing in the middle of the garden, he finally joined her. His attention was caught by the ring's strange design.

"Looks like some kind of Mexican brand," he said.

She held it up for his inspection. "It is called a *rúbrica*. In the old days, the Moors wore rings with designs on them . . . their initials, or something signifying their house

. . . and, instead of signing their name, stamped this in hot wax on the paper, forming sort of a seal. The Moors carried it into Spain in their conquest. The design in this ring has been handed down through our family for generations."

"You're full of stories."

"You don't have to restrain yourself so nobly. You've been looking at me that way ever since *Cabo* mentioned Captain Velasco, up there on the mountain."

"I don't deny it. When you first told me the legend of El Renegado, you were very careful not to name the captain who betrayed his people. How are you descended from him?"

"There are many versions of the legend of El Renegado," she said. "One of them is a belief, as persistent as it is false, that the descendants of Captain Velasco are back in the Patagonias somewhere, a race, a people to themselves, really. Not true half-breeds, because the mating of Velasco and the Indian girl was so many centuries before, that the division of blood has almost been lost. They are supposed to be renegades, as he was, bandits, murderers, veritable ogres, capable of appalling atrocities, holding the simpletons of Tintown and the other settlements outside the basin in constant fear. You know how a thing like that can grow through the centuries. Every deed of violence within a thousand miles is attributed to this band."

"And there's no truth in it?"

"I am the only descendant of Velasco," she said. "He did have children, but they drifted down off the mountains into this basin years ago, adopting the customs and language of the Spaniards who had come into New Mexico by then. One of them did such service to the Spanish Crown that he was pardoned for his ancestor's crime, and granted the land this *hacienda* occupies."

He studied her face, finding logic in those curiously haunted eyes. He leaned toward her, a vagrant smile catching at his mouth for the first time.

"Will you forgive my suspicions?"

"I'm used to them. It is the usual reaction to the name, Velasco. I didn't realize how bad it really was till father died. It left me completely alone here."

She sat, staring moodily at the flagstones, and he had to say something, anything. "How did he die?" For a moment, he thought a cloud had passed before the sun. The shadow crossing her face was that palpable. Then, instinctively, he glanced toward El Renegado. "You aren't thinking of the . . . the . . . ?"

"The curse?" she finished, head lifting in some sharp defiance. "You sound like your brother. I thought you were different. I thought you were sensitive to those things. Do you know how old I am? Twenty-five. Do you know how many days I've heard laughter in this house? Not one. In all my life, not one!"

She was standing now, staring at the wall, fists clenched at her sides, giving vent to some violent release that had been gathering force for a long time. "Do you know how much pain and tragedy and death I've seen? A grandfather paralyzed when he fell from his horse, sitting for ten years like a stone statue faced toward the mountain. A grandmother burned to death in the stables. A mother killed when she was thrown downstairs by her husband in a drunken rage. A son killing him for it. A lifetime of loneliness because my name is Velasco. Not a man in the towns around here has had the courage to look at me, for fear of the curse. How can I help but think of that curse, when I say anything, do anything, remember anything?"

He saw she was on the verge of crying and got to his feet sharply, catching her. She turned to him with a hunger that surprised him, molding her body into the circle of his arms, and then he was answering the hunger, pulling her against him with a savage passion he had not known himself capable of, cupping a hand under her chin to lift her face. His lips were still on hers when he heard someone call her name.

"Tina? Tina?"

The voice was unmistakable. It caused him something close to pain to pull his mouth away and turn toward the sound. All the romance of Erin had always given Farris Shane his way with women, and it was so typical of him to make a flourish of it that way, ignoring the half-open gate in the *zaguán* to come vaulting over the top of the adobe wall itself, from the back of his horse outside. Mouth still open from calling her name, he had already seen them before he landed.

His knees bent with the weight of his body striking the ground, then straightened, and he was staring at them with eyes already blackened by storm.

"Colin?" he said, in a small, unbelieving way. "Colin," he repeated, his voice now hoarse, angry.

"Farris," cried Colin, releasing the woman abruptly. "Don't be a fool."

"I *have been* a fool," said Farris, his tone so thick with anger he could hardly speak. "It was you. Behind my back. Knowing how I felt about her, and meeting her like this."

"Farris. . . ."

"I told you, Colin, how it would be."

The rest of it was lost as he rushed Colin in that blind, roaring rage. Colin tried to wheel aside, but Farris spun him against the wall. He caught Colin there, doubling him over with a vicious punch to the groin. Gripped in the nauseating pain of it, Colin would have fallen to the ground except for Farris there in front of him, pinning him against the wall.

Dimly, somewhere down in the pain-filled recesses of him, he realized that, if Farris hit him once more, he would be through. With Farris's body against him, holding him up, he felt the surge of muscle, shifting away from his own left side, that told him of his brother's right arm being brought back for a second blow.

His long legs found purchase, and he shoved with all the strength of them, just as Farris struck. Tripping backward, Farris's blow lost all its force, falling weakly against Colin's shoulder. Colin kept shoving, his arms wound about the man's waist. Farris came up against something with a tumbling crash of wood and stone. He seemed to surge upward in Colin's arms, as if something had lifted his feet off the ground. Then all the tension left Farris's body. He fell backward. There was another sharp crack, something sickening this time.

It must have been Farris's head striking that oaken bench, for he lay sprawled on his back just beside it, darkening the flagstones with his blood. Colin swayed above him, staring at the growing red stain. Then, face twisting, he dropped to his knees beside his brother.

"Farris?" he said, in a weak, husky voice. There was no answer. "Farris?" Lifting the head up. "Farris?" Seeing the eyes roll open, white and sightless and dead.

"I'll . . . I'll get some water," whispered Tina, standing above them.

Colin dropped his brother's head back. "He doesn't need any water," he told her, in a voice that did not belong to him. For a moment, he thought the blood had spread across all the patio floor, to darken it that way. Then he felt the chill of the garden, and turned his face upward. The woman was looking in that direction, too, an ominous fulfillment torturing her face. The sun was setting behind the Patagonias, and the shadow of El Renegado lay black as Farris's blood across the whole garden.

Six 🌵

Consciousness of a great heat came to Colin. He tried to open his eyes. There was blinding brightness. He realized he was on his back, and rolled over. The grit of earth scraped his belly. He got to his hands and knees, opening his eyes again. He saw that there was barren land about him — great, ruddy rocks and steep, sandy barrancas. He had a dim, whirling memory. Farris was in it somehow. He sat down, holding his head in his hands, trying to think.

It returned then, like a blow, memory of the fight in the garden. Farris dead? He raised his head, unable to believe it. He was a murderer, then. Of his own brother.

In this torture, he stared around him, trying to make out where he was. There seemed to be mountains all about him, stark, barren, unworldly. He thought, for a moment, of a dream. But it was too real for that. More memory came, filtering in painfully, dim and tantalizing. He could almost see the man stumbling out through that *zaguán*, eyes blank and staring in the madness of realizing what he had done. Was it he? He had wandered, then. He had run from the scene of his crime and wandered to this spot, too crazed with grief and guilt to have any lucid memory of it.

He looked at his shirt. It was in tatters. How long had he been wandering? He felt his beard. It was a rough stubble an inch long. It had been days. He tried to rise, fell back. On his second attempt he made it.

Now he knew a burning thirst, and began walking, aimlessly, hands outstretched, unable to see half the time because the sun was so bright. He stumbled and fell many times. The one thought in his mind was water. Then something else began replacing that. He felt his arms twitch, as if tensing to strike something. His lips moved in someone's name. He saw a face before him, and saw himself hitting at it. Farris. Farris, on the ground before him, with the blood darkening the flagstones. A scream of anguish escaped him, and he dug his fists into his eyes to escape the vision, running from it, running with small, animal sobbing sounds, stumbling and falling again, losing sanity before the persistent, maddening memory that blended with reality until he could not tell them apart.

He ran on down the sandy, desolate slope,

a tattered, babbling figure, sinking finally into the same apathetic state that had led him wandering so long with no memory of it.

When he became lucid again, the heat was gone, the burning thirst. He knew a great sense of coolness. Above him was a ceiling, laced with the herring-bone pattern of the willow shoots they laid beneath the foot of earth forming the roofs of their adobe houses. Under these stretched the *viga* poles that were the rafters, forming dim, smoke-blackened lines from wall to wall. Then it was the face, the greasy, bland, grinning face, and the man squatting back on his heels.

"Pajarero."

"*Sí*," smiled the bird-catcher. "I found you wandering the Patagonias. Loco in the head. *Ai*. Does it torture one so, to kill his own brother?"

Colin's face twisted. "You know?"

"The whole basin knows," said Pajarero. "You and he fought in the woman's garden, and he died in the shadow of El Renegado." He seemed to be looking beyond Colin. "Did you ever wonder why it was you who lived, and not he?"

Colin tried to sit up. "How do you mean?"

"He was the one who scoffed at

Renegado. Sometimes the unbelievers are punished in strange ways for their heresy."

Colin's efforts to rise brought a chorus of squawks from the birds in the cages around the room. The bird-catcher rose from his hunkers and fluttered around from one to another, calming them.

"Quiet, Pepita. *Caramba*. Are you old women, that you screech at a mouse? Silence, García. That does not befit a gentleman."

Finally he had them quieted down, and he shuffled over to a pot of stew simmering over one of the pot fires on the adobe hearth, ladling out a bowl for Colin, muttering into his fat jowls. Colin sat amid the fetid sheepskin pallets, gulping the stew ravenously, following it with a dozen cold tortillas piled on a plate.

"We're in Tintown?" he asked Pajarero, at last.

"In the Patagonias," said the man.

"I thought you lived in Tintown."

"I live wherever my travels take me," said the man grumpily.

Colin studied the man. "Why did you take me in, Pajarero?"

Something withdrew in that round, greasy face. "You would have died out there. You had the fever. This is your first clear head in three days. I been nursing you like a baby."

Colin moved again, feeling the weakness in him. Even talk cost him an effort. But he had to know. "Why, though, Pajarero?" he insisted. "You know how I stand with Nacho. I think he's quite capable of killing you for taking me in this way. Don't you?"

The man squinted, as if in pain at the name, and Colin understood it. "Maybe because I saved you from him that first time?" he asked.

"Well, well," muttered Pajarero, "so I am not so noble . . . so I had a reason for taking you in. Maybe you are the only one in the valley who has opposed Nacho and lived. I heard about that business with the guns. *Poom!*" He made a gesture of drawing a gun, index finger pointed. "So fast nobody saw it come out. So fast Nacho started first and still didn't have anything free in time."

"And you're hiding from him?" asked Colin.

The man made vague, shrugging movements with his shoulders and arms, pouting and muttering incoherently, moving over to pour coffee he had put on to boil.

"Why?" asked Colin. "Why was he trying to kill you that first day?"

"How would I know?" said Pajarero, turning away.

"Does he run a gang back here in the Patagonias?"

"I don't know *nada* about nothing."

"You mean you're afraid to tell. How is Tina mixed up in it? What is Nacho to her?"

"*Dios,*" exploded the man, waving his hand so violently he spilled the coffee. "Haven't I saved your life? Is that not enough? What do you want? The history of the New World? Drink your coffee and be thankful I have found it in my groveling little soul to do this much. Now, rest a while. I have to go and get water from the *tinaja.*"

A *tinaja* was a natural rock sink in which rain water collected during the wet season. Colin expected the man back in a few moments, but time stretched out to an hour, two hours. He was stirring feebly within the stifling hovel, worried about the bird-catcher, when the man's grimy, weary face poked through the low door.

"*Agua,*" he grinned. "Enough to last a couple of days if we do not wash."

"Do you mean to tell me it's that far away?" muttered Colin.

"Over two mountains," chuckled Pajarero.

"You really are holed in," said Colin.

"*El diablo* himself could not find us," smiled the man secretively. "The Patagonias

298

themselves are so inaccessible that no more than a dozen men have penetrated them in the last century, and this is the most inaccessible spot in all the Patagonias."

Colin knew it was useless to ask the man again why he was so afraid of Nacho. He settled down to recovering, dozing most of that first day of restored consciousness, moving about some the second. He began to brood during that time, about Farris, sinking into a black, ugly mood that lasted for hours.

"But it was not your fault," Pajarero pleaded with him, over and over. "You did not mean to kill him. You were only defending yourself. It was an accident, *amigo,* that bench."

When this argument failed, the man would try to amuse Colin by babbling about his experiences in Yucatán, or Darien, or some other forgotten section of Mexico, hunting birds. It helped, somehow. There was a naïve simplicity to Pajarero, for all his travels, all his strange, exotic knowledge, that lifted Colin out of his depression. But there was always something behind the talk — in those quiet, expressive eyes of Pajarero's, in the way he watched Colin sometimes — a sense of pendant waiting. Colin had regained most of his strength by the third time Pajarero had to go for water.

After the man had left, Colin went outside the door, hunkering down against the wall, squinting against the haze of heat the sun brought.

It was just a little, one-room, adobe *jacal,* walls crumbling with age, a corral of cottonwood poles behind, holding Pajarero's jackass and a couple of mangy horses. On every side, the mountains lifted their jagged, barren steeps to the sky, utterly devoid of vegetation. A buzzard circled high above. The silence had a palpable pressure. Shadows lengthened slowly, crawling like black fingers across the rocks to touch Colin. They brought him a sudden chill. He stirred, realizing how long Pajarero had been gone this time.

He went inside, lying on the fetid sheep-skins. He must have dozed, for when he awoke, it was night. A loafer wolf filled the darkness with its mourning. Colin moved restlessly about the building, looking off in the direction Pajarero always took.

When the moon began to rise, shedding a pale, unworldly light over the peaks, he went inside again, pawing through the sheepskins till he found where Pajarero had put his Paterson. He shoved the gun in behind his belt buckle and went to get one of the horses. There was an ancient Mexican tree-saddle on the top pole of the corral. With this on the beast, he set off up the trail he had watched the bird-catcher take.

It was so rocky the hoofs left no mark, and he soon lost his way. He was on the point of turning back when he realized the horse was tugging at the reins, trying to face the other way. A thirsty animal had some sense of water many miles away, and he gave the animal its head. The horse went at a deliberate walk, as true as if it had traveled the trail all its life, carrying him across one of the knife-like peaks and into another valley. The wolf was still howling off in the distance somewhere, when the other sound joined it. A faint mewing, like a sick cat.

He saw it, finally. Pajarero had been tied to a jumping cholla. Some of the longer spines had thrust clear through his body at the sides and other narrower portions. His shirt front was rusty with blood. There were the charred coals of a fire at one side, with several half-burnt stalks of Spanish dagger. Jumping off his horse and going to his knees beside the man, Colin saw what they had been used for. Pajarero's eyes had been burned out.

"*Agua,*" whispered the fat, little Mexican, moving his head from side to side. "*Ruego de alma mía, señor,* I can hear you . . . help me. . . ." He broke off, chest lifting with his sharp breath. "Nacho?"

"No, Pajarero," said Colin gently. "It's Colin. Take it easy and I'll have you off this."

"No, no," bleated the man, like a weak child. "I die soon. Do not cause me more pain."

Colin settled back to his heels, holding the man. "Why did Nacho do this?"

"He wanted me to tell where you were." He made a ghastly attempt at a smile. "I'm proud of myself, *señor.* When you go through Tintown, do me the favor of telling the other bird-catchers that Nacho is not so terrible. He could not even make Pajarero talk."

"This wasn't why he was trying to kill you that first time."

"I suppose not."

"Can't you tell me now, Pajarero? Who is Nacho?"

"There are some things even the wind dare not whisper, *señor.*"

"You're protecting Tina. It has something to do with her."

"Does it, *señor?*"

"Why did you stay in the basin, knowing Nacho would kill you?"

"I have traveled two continents in the

quest of rare birds," said the man weakly. "There was one rarest, most beautiful of all . . . which I desired more than any other in the world. But I am only a fat, stupid little *pajarero*, a comical clown of a bird-catcher, and it was denied me. All I could do was flutter about outside its cage."

Colin's throat twitched as he realized whom Pajarero meant. He remembered the dog-like devotion in the man's eyes that first time they had seen Tina, remembered how Pajarero had tried to kiss the hem of her skirt, on his knees. At the time, it had been almost amusing to Colin. The full pathos of it struck him now.

"*Ai*," said Pajarero, at his silence. "You see, now. And if I had it to do over again, it would be no different. For but one more look at her, I would take ten times this torture. They kept trying to get you to go, didn't they?"

"Tina?"

"She. Your mother. Even I told you how foolish you were to stay, once. And yet, you stayed. You had seen her, too. We are not very different underneath, *señor*. Your plumage may be more brilliant, but inside it is the same. I would ask you, as a dying favor, to leave now. But I know how useless that would be. You will stay and be killed, because you have seen her. Renegado is fulfilled in strange ways."

He leaned back against the cactus, greasy face contorting in some last spasm of pain. Then he sank down, and the shallow breathing stopped. Staring down at the round, fat face, Colin felt a tear begin rolling down his cheek. He was crying. The pain of his anguish was the more intense because he could make no sound.

Later, he untied the man and gathered rocks for a cairn, piling them over his body. Then he gathered up the gum-pitched *morrales* Pajarero had been carrying the water in, slinging them over the withers of his horse, and set off on the trail. The rock and talus had given way to parched earth here, which recorded the prints of four horses faithfully. By the moonlight, it was not too hard to follow.

Seven 🐃

The mountains seemed to rise and fall about Colin, before him, behind him, like a gigantic sea, as he traversed peak after peak, valley after valley. He came to vegetation, ocotillo spreading from an arroyo like a fountain of gold, candlewood spouting a torch of flame from its spidery wands. And then, ahead, El Renegado, appearing suddenly behind a nearer range, like a great, somber skull, thrusting up out of its cerements.

The awe it brought struck Colin so forcibly he felt a vague nausea. It caused him great effort to push on, keeping his attention on those tracks. He knew he was nearing the basin now, and wondered if they were seeking him at his house. He plunged through creosote, yellow with flower, into a steep arroyo, still on the trail, finding it again as it came from the creosote into the sandy wash. Then the walls of the arroyo echoed and reverberated to crazy, cackling laughter, and that voice filled with the archaic accent of Castilian.

"Here is an *indio, capitán.* I have an *indio, capitán. . . .*"

Recognizing the voice, Colin pulled up his jaded horse, staring about him. A gun crashed, and his horse leaped into the air with a scream. Colin threw himself off the thrashing animal before it went down, pulling his gun as he fell.

He struck heavily, rolling through deep sand to come against mesquite with a loud crackle. Stunned, he crawled into the bushes.

He could hear horses galloping back down the arroyo now. Three riders burst around its winding curve into the broadening wash, with Nacho in the lead, spurring his horse brutally. Colin raised to his knees in the bushes, holding his gun out till he had it point-blank on the man's body, and fired. Nacho shouted in pain, pitching upward and backward off his animal, with arms spread-eagled to the sky.

Colin saw the other two men wheel in the saddle toward him, trying to pull their horses up and fire all at once. It was too fast and too confused to be sure of hitting the men now, and Colin lowered his gun to shoot their horses out from under them, one after the other. The first animal went down by the front, tumbling its rider over the head, and the second veered off sideways suddenly, crashing into the rocky slope of the arroyo, and whipping his man out of the saddle. The man flopped down to the bottom of that slope like a doll with all the sand gone, and lay motionless there. Farther back, in the broader bottom of the arroyo, the other man lay on his back, calling softly in pain.

"Nacho . . . Nacho . . . come get me, damn you. My leg's broke . . . my leg's broke. . . ."

This had all taken no more than a minute, but, as Colin's attention was swept back to the spot where he had shot Nacho, he could not see the man. Blood stained the sand and made an unmistakable trail into the creosote on the other side of the arroyo. Colin searched those bushes for some sign of movement, unwilling to move, with The Corporal still somewhere up above him.

One of the horses he had shot lay kicking and writhing in the sand, and the other had fallen to its side, in death. Farther up the arroyo, where Colin had first entered it, was Nacho's horse. Nacho rode with split reins, and they had dropped to the earth. He must have been trained for ground-hitching, as most Mexican animals were, for he had spooked that far from the excitement, and then halted, fiddling around nervously.

Colin wanted that horse the worst way, with his own animal down. He decided at last that he had to find The Corporal before he could expose himself, and turned to worm his way through the cover of rocks and bushes up his side of the arroyo, seeking the spot from which the crazy old man had shot his horse.

"Nacho," called the man, from down at the bottom. "Come and get me, damn you . . . come and get me, my leg's broke, I say."

Almost at the lip of the arroyo, Colin heard a dim, muttering sound. He wormed through mesquite toward it. Through this brush, finally, he made out The Corporal crouched down over that ancient match-lock, fumbling with the pan. Colin must have made some rustle in the mesquite, for the old man's head jerked up. Colin felt his gun move abruptly to cover The Corporal. The man leered blankly at him.

"Have you got a match, comrade?" he asked. "The Indians are down in the valley, and I'm out of matches."

"You damned old fool," muttered Colin. He still kept his gun on the man, knowing a frustrating indecision. Before it left him, there was some movement down in the arroyo to attract his attention. It was in the creosote, up at the end where Nacho's horse had halted. The animal began fiddling again down there, ears pricked. Colin could not help raise up as he saw a man pull himself out of the creosote, clutching at a stirrup. The horse tried to dance away, but the man caught a leather, hauling himself erect.

It was Nacho. He must have crawled through the brush from where he had fallen to get his horse, knowing that Colin was looking for him. Colin started moving, trying to find a position that would clear the man for his gun. But Nacho was mounting on the opposite side of his horse. In desperation, Colin aimed at the animal.

"Watch out, *capitán!*" screamed The Corporal, from behind Colin. "The *bribón* is going to shoot you . . . !"

Colin half turned in time to see the old man jumping at him, that gun clubbed. He ducked under it, throwing The Corporal over his shoulder. Nacho was racing down the arroyo now. Colin snapped a shot at him, but he was going too fast, and too far away.

Colin wheeled to where The Corporal's horse stood, a mangy crow-bait with trailing reins. The animal did not even shy when he ran up on it. He had to boot it unmercifully to get any movement. He passed The Corporal, trying to climb back up the slope from where Colin had thrown him, and then he slid the horse down the bank into the arroyo. Pushing the horse, he reached the end of this to run out into a series of benches with Nacho in sight, crossing them.

Colin knew there was no use trying to catch Nacho, on this old nag, but he felt no desire to. It was a certainty in him, where the man was going, and he figured Nacho would be more sure to keep in that direction if he thought he was not followed. Colin allowed his horse to slow down, until Nacho ran out of sight into the timber at the footslopes of El Renegado.

With the mountain there, Colin knew where he was, now, and he took a southwesterly direction, not even bothering to follow Nacho's trail directly. El Renegado brooded over him the whole distance, some malignant portent in its air of patient, sinister waiting. He was tense in the saddle, with its spell, when he came out onto the flats of the basin. The Velasco *hacienda* was ahead of him. He approached it through the cottonwoods growing in the river bottom. This cover brought him right up against the high adobe wall surrounding the place. Down this wall about fifty feet was a broad *zaguán,* the logical gate to use for anyone coming from the direction Colin had. And before it, on the ground, even at this distance, he saw the bloodstains.

Thought of Farris was in his mind, as he lifted himself to a standing position in the saddle, against the wall, grasping the tiles on top and hoisting his body over. A weeping willow dropped its foliage over the wall here, and in this momentary screen he reloaded his gun from the handful of shells he always carried in his pocket.

After this was done, he found himself unwilling to move. He was torn between a deep reluctance to find Nacho with Tina, and a bitter desire to finish this up, for Pajarero, for Farris, for his mother.

He forced himself from the screen of willow, dropping off the wall. There was a row of sheds ahead of him, filled with the muted stamp and snort of horses, and he realized he was in the back end of a stable yard. He moved through the reek of rotten hay and droppings, around the end of this row of adobe stalls. This brought him to the main yard, into which the *zaguán* opened. It was lit by flaring torches, and Nacho's horse stood hipshot and blowing next to a half-open door.

Colin stepped to the door, listened a moment. There were muffled voices from far within. Carefully, he pushed the portal open. He was staring down a long hall, lined with the niches in which they placed their carved wooden saints. Blood stains made a trail down the floor to another door at the end, partly ajar. Colin made his way to this. The voices seemed to lift away from him now. He saw beyond the second door a great room, lit by a dozen candles, filling the candelabra of beaten silver on a great oak table. The light drank in mauve *savanarillas* hanging on the walls, seemed to catch up the faded red of a Chimayo blanket draped across the adobe *banco* that ran all the way around the room to form a foot-high bench molded in against the wall.

At the far side of the room, a stairway rose, railed in wrought iron, tarnished and rusted with age. Finally he could wait no longer. He pushed the door open with a boot. Nothing happened. He stepped into the room, ducking over back of the table. Still nothing. He darted for the wall by the stairway. He was almost to the corner, where it would afford him cover from the steps higher up, when a shot rocked the room.

It caught him across the side of his thigh, filling him with the hot, inchoate sense of a burning, lashing blow, twisting him halfway around. His run carried him up against the wall at that corner, however, half falling across the adobe *banco*. With this for support, he bent forward and sent a shot up the dark stairwell.

There was the scream of a ricochet, a sharp, withdrawing movement up there. He took that indication of retreat to jump onto the stairs, firing upward again, seeing the dim shape above. There was one answering shot, ripping adobe off in pale flakes from the wall at the side of his head. He fired a third time with the body fully in his sights.

"*¡Por Dios!*" screamed Nacho, pain rending his voice. Then there was a heavy, thumping, sliding sound, as of someone dragging themselves down a wall. Colin's leg would bear his weight no longer, and he went down on the stairs before he reached the top. Lying there, with light from below still strong enough to see, he made out that the bullet had struck the great outer muscle of his thigh, going down in a long, deep flesh wound to come out at his knee on the same side.

"Nacho?" called a woman's voice, from up there. "Nacho, please. . . ."

It was Tina, her voice driving Colin to crawl on up the stairs. His head came over the top step, and he could see down another long hall. Light from its end was blocked off by the woman's body. He saw a low niche in the wall above him, and reached up to clutch at its edge, pulling down the wooden *santo* it contained as he struggled up. Tina reached him then, trying to keep him from going on.

"Colin, please, you can't do it . . . please!"

"Maybe you didn't see what he did to Pajarero," said Colin, twisting inexorably around her.

Tina's struggles to hold him became more violent. "Pajarero? I can't help it . . . you mustn't . . . not Nacho."

"If I had more guts, it would be you, too," he said, tearing loose. He almost fell, then put himself into a headlong run that carried him in a stumbling, hurtling passage down the hall. He came to the head of the stairs, illumined by light from below, and saw Nacho on the landing, halfway down. The man turned, raising his gun. But Colin had his held level, waist high, and all he had to do was pull the trigger. It made a deafening crash. Nacho was punched heavily back against the wall. Then he pitched forward, rolling down the stairs to the bottom. Colin went down after him to make sure.

Nacho's dead right hand was thrust outward, a ring on the curling fourth finger. Colin stared at the design on it, the Velasco *rúbrica*. The rustle of skirts brought his head around. Tina was staring at the ring with wide, tortured eyes.

"Are you satisfied now?" she asked.

He looked up at her with frowning eyes. "He's a Velasco?"

"My brother."

"And I thought . . . ," muttered Colin, staring blankly at Nacho. "I thought. . . ."

"You thought he was my lover?" she finished, when he would not go on.

Colin nodded dully. "You mentioned your father throwing your mother downstairs in a drunken rage, and a son killing him for it."

"That was Nacho," she said. "It changed him, somehow. We tried not to blame him for killing Father. It was such a terrible thing Father had done. But it twisted Nacho. He had been such a good boy before. He turned into something wild, like an animal, running off into the Patagonias and gathering that bunch of filthy, crazy *bribónes* around him, like The Corporal, taking advantage of the Renegado legend about the descendants of Velasco being back in there, just to maraud the countryside. And then he would come back for a little time, and be the boy he had been, giving me the company and companionship I craved so here, and I would know the hope that he was changing. That's why I wanted you to leave. He was still my brother. Can you understand the position I was in? I knew that one of you would kill the other, if you stayed. From the first, it was obvious. He was my brother *and* my lover. Isn't that a happy choice? And now . . . now?" She sank to her knees beside Nacho, the tears running silently down her face. "Now one of you has killed the other."

"No wonder Pajarero wouldn't tell me your connection with Nacho," murmured Colin. "And it was you who stampeded those cattle, and Farris found you up on Renegado that day?"

"Yes," she nodded dully. "Ichahi and I did it. Do you blame me?" He was silent so long she raised her head, meeting his eyes, seeing what was in them. "I didn't know Farris was coming that day, though, Colin. I didn't plan *that*. You can't believe I did."

In a sudden, impulsive way, unable to put his answer into words, he reached out for her, lifting her to her feet, encircling her with his arms. For a long time they stood that close, finding comfort in the nearness, until he finally sensed the subtle tension flowing into her body. He felt as if something had touched him from behind, and realized they were no longer standing in the dawn sunlight. A shadow had dropped across them. They both turned as one, staring at the mountain, forming its somber, brooding silhouette against the morning sunrise. Tina made a small, tortured sound.

"You've got to get that out of your system," he said. "Nacho was causing everything as much as the mountain."

"Did he cause your mother's death?" she asked. "Or Farris's?"

He felt something within him contract at the thought of Farris, and could not help its showing on his face, that dark, mystic sensitivity to the spell of the mountain.

"You'll take me away from here, Colin? You won't try to stay here any longer? You feel it as deeply as I do?"

"Where I am going, Tina, you cannot come."

"But where are you going?" she asked, arching away from him in sudden defiance.

"If you will show me where Farris's body is buried, I shall move him, so he can rest beside our mother's grave."

"And then?" she asked.

"Then," he said sadly, but with a dim light of hope in his eyes, "then I will begin all over again. I told you the night our mother died, Tina. *We* aren't leaving the valley." With the chill of that shadow in his very bones, tears now again in his eyes, he repeated the words slowly. "No, Tina. Where I am going, you cannot come."

LES SAVAGE, JR. was born in Alhambra, California, and grew up in Los Angeles. His first published story was "Bullets and Bullwhips" accepted by the prestigious magazine, Street & Smith's *Western Story*. Almost ninety more magazine stories followed, all set on the American frontier, many of them published in Fiction House magazines such as *Frontier Stories* and *Lariat Story Magazine* where Savage became a superstar with his name on many covers. His first novel, *Treasure of the Brasada*, appeared from Simon & Schuster in 1947. Due to his preference for historical accuracy, Savage often ran into problems with book editors in the 1950s who were concerned about marriages between his protagonists and women of different races — commonplace on the real frontier but not in much Western fiction in that decade. Savage died young, at thirty-five, from complications arising out of hereditary diabetes and elevated cholesterol. Such noteworthy titles as *Silver Street Woman* (1954), *Return to Warbow* (1956), and *Beyond Wind River* (1958) have become classics of Western fiction. However, as a result of the censorship imposed on many of his works, only now are they being fully restored by returning to the author's original manuscripts. Among Savage's finest Western stories are *Fire Dance at Spider Rock* (Five Star Westerns, 1995), *Copper Bluffs* (Circle V Westerns, 1996), *Medicine Wheel* (Five Star Westerns, 1996), *Coffin Gap* (Five Star Westerns, 1997), *Phantoms in the Night* (Five Star Westerns, 1998), and *The Bloody Quarter* (Five Star Westerns, 1999). Much as Stephen Crane before him, while he wrote, the shadow of his imminent death grew longer and longer across his young life, and he knew that, if he was going to do it at all, he would have to do it quickly. He did it well, better than almost anyone who wrote Western and frontier fiction, ever. Now that his novels and stories are being restored to what he had intended them to be, his achievement irradiated by his powerful and profoundly sensitive imagination will be with us always, as he had wanted it to be, as he had so rushed against time and mortality that it might be.

We hope you have enjoyed this Large Print book. Other Thorndike Press or Chivers Press Large Print books are available at your library or directly from the publishers.

For more information about current and upcoming titles, please call or write, without obligation, to:

Thorndike Press
P.O. Box 159
Thorndike, Maine 04986 USA
Tel. (800) 223-1244
Tel. (800) 223-6121

OR

Chivers Press Limited
Windsor Bridge Road
Bath BA2 3AX
England
Tel. (0225) 335336

All our Large Print titles are designed for easy reading, and all our books are made to last.